THE BLOOD GUARD

Carter Roy is an award-winning short-story writer and memoirist for adults who has published more than a half-dozen pieces in journals and anthologies. This is his debut novel. He lives in New York City.

THE BLOOD GUARD

CARTER ROY

SCHOLASTIC

First published in the UK in 2014 by Scholastic Children's Books
An imprint of Scholastic Ltd
Euston House, 24 Eversholt Street
London NW1 1DB, UK
Registered office: Westfield Road, Southam, Warwickshire, CV47 0RA
SCHOLASTIC and associated logos are trademarks and/
or registered trademarks of Scholastic Inc.

First published in the US by Amazon Publishing, 2014
First published in the UK by Scholastic Ltd, 2014

INKHOUSE

The right of Carter Roy to be identified as the author
of this work has been asserted by him.

ISBN 978 1 4071 36998

A CIP catalogue record for this book
is available from the British Library

Printed and bound by CPI Group (UK) Ltd, Croydon, CR0 4YY
Papers used by Scholastic Children's Books are made from wood
grown in sustainable forests

1 3 5 7 9 10 8 6 4 2

Though J. Seward Johnson, Jr.'s sculpture called *The Awakening* is very
real, the author has taken liberty with its size, dimensions and even current
location. These days it can be found not at Hains Point in DC,
but at National Harbor in nearby Maryland.

FOR BETH,
ONLY EVERYTHING

PLAYING WITH FIRE

It wasn't *me* who burned down our house.

I wasn't even supposed to be there. I'd been sent home from school with a fever, and I'd taken a nap. Next thing I knew, flames were licking under my door and white smoke was filling the room. Pretty soon after that I was hugging the brownstone wall outside my third-floor bedroom window, wishing I'd put on some clothes first.

It was snowing. Hard. And the ledge I was standing on was slippery. Below me, the entire front of the house was ablaze, long tongues of fire stretching from every window.

So I went the other way. Up.

Scaling a burning building in a snowstorm in pyjamas

and bare feet? Not my idea of fun. But sometimes you don't really have a choice.

Eventually, I reached the edge of our roof and hoisted myself over. *Safe*, I thought. The tarred surface was nice and warm under the soles of my feet. I almost felt like I could lie down and go to sleep again.

And then I snapped wide awake. *It's warm*, I thought. *In a snowstorm.*

I took off running.

I'd barely leaped across to the neighbour's when our roof fell in. It made a plume of pretty sparks that shot up high into the air and then rained down on the neighbourhood, the ash mixing with the snow.

I stood and watched, wondering what I was going to tell my mom.

It all seemed unreal – not just because I was feverish, barefoot, covered in soot and wearing singed pyjamas. But because our house was the only one in the row to catch fire.

A professional job, the investigators called it later, but that was just a guess. They never found evidence of arson. And they couldn't figure out a motive for why my parents or I would want to destroy our own home. So after a while, they gave up and labelled it a freak accident.

We moved to a new place in a new neighbourhood, in a totally new state. I went to a new school with new kids who didn't accuse me of being the boy who played with fire.

I figured I'd survived the worst moment of my life. Nothing else that happened to me could ever come close to being as awful as that one day.

But I was wrong. Boy was I ever.

CHAPTER ONE

TRUST NO ONE

Call me Ronan.

It's my middle name. My first is *Evelyn* and my last is *Truelove*, which is kind of a spectacular bummer on all fronts, because I'm a guy. My mom's uncle Evelyn was from Great Britain. Maybe that name doesn't sound weird for a boy there? He had a house on a huge wooded lake in northern Michigan. So because my mom liked paddling a canoe there when she was nine, she gave me a first name that sounds like a girl's.

I can't even begin to explain how wrong this is.

My name gets me a whole lot of attention. By the time I got to kindergarten, I was used to the teasing; it was the fights that were new. This enormous kid named Dennis

Gault decided he wanted my lunch box. "Give it here, *Evelyn*," he said. Dennis was only in second grade, but he looked like a giant, with fists as big as cantaloupes.

It wasn't much of a lunch box — just a cheap plastic *Dragon Ball Z* thing — but I wasn't about to hand it over. "Don't call me Evelyn," I replied.

I got home an hour later, lunch box gone, blood running from my nose. I don't know what I thought my mom would do. Call the principal and complain, maybe.

Instead, she enrolled me in judo. "It's time you learned how to fight," she said.

"I don't *want* to fight!" I said.

"Cut the whining. This will be good for you."

I was *five*.

I'm thirteen now, and because of my mom, I've taken everything from judo to aikido, Krav Maga to kendo. (Kendo is a Japanese martial art in which you beat up your opponent with a long stick. It looks like good times until someone starts whacking you back.) And Mom didn't just sign me up for self-defence. She's had me take classes in swing dance and horseback riding and wilderness survival training and — well, she makes sure that I am always busy.

Thanks to all the classes, these days I know how to

take care of myself in a fight. These days, no one bullies me. And no one calls me Evelyn.

Most of the time no one calls me anything at all.

I don't have all that many friends at my new school. When we moved to Connecticut after the fire, the kids already had their friendships locked down. It didn't help much that I'm always skipping off after school to take weird classes in fencing or metalworking or advanced gymnastics. I mean, imagine explaining to your new maybe-friend that you can't hang out and play PS3 because you have to pull on a leotard and perfect your dismount from the parallel bars. Pretty soon no one invites you to anything.

Gymnastics was where I was headed the afternoon when everything started. School had just let out for the day and the halls were buzzing. I stood at my locker and listened to the kids around me talk about an end-of-year pool party that a popular eighth-grader was throwing that weekend. Just about everyone had been invited.

Everyone but me.

I swapped my algebra textbook for social studies, then stuffed it into my backpack on top of my leotard.

"You going to hit Cassie's swim thing on Saturday?" Nathan Romaneck was in my honours classes. He was a little bit of a dweeb – his crew cut and old T-shirt made him look like an eight-year-old – but he was one of the few kids who was sort of kind of like a friend.

"Lost my invite," I said.

"I wasn't invited either," he said, shrugging. "But I'm going anyway. The crowd there will be big enough that we'll be invisible."

"I'd love to go," I started to say, "but I've—"

"Got trapeze class or whatever until eight. And then fencing Sunday morning," he said. "I know. Your mom calls the shots and you have to do as she tells you. Want to get into a good college, blah blah blah."

"It's not like that, Nate," I said, but we both knew he was right. My mom kept me aggressively overscheduled. I wasn't always crazy about it, but I also didn't mind. You don't care as much about being an outsider if you're always busy.

I closed my locker and was fighting my way through the flood of kids in front of the building when I heard someone call my name.

"Evelyn Ronan Truelove!"

Only one person calls me that.

My mom.

She was leaning against her yellow VW bug, parked

in clear violation of the TEACHERS ONLY sign. She wore a blue men's dress shirt with the sleeves rolled to her elbows and paint-spattered blue jeans, and her long black hair was tied back in a messy ponytail. My mom stands out in a crowd, mostly because of the burning intensity of her eyes: when she is looking at you, it's like the sun shines on you alone. No one and nothing else exists.

"Are you here to drive me to gymnastics?" I asked as I walked over. It was strange to see her here – she works full-time as a museum curator and isn't usually done early enough to pick me up from school. I swung my backpack into the VW and climbed in. "Because I'm good with walking there, honest."

"Special treat," she said, glancing quickly to either side. I looked too, but there was nothing much to see, just the usual end-of-the-school-day business: hundreds of kids pouring out in a noisy flood, a line of yellow buses idling in the far lot. "Buckle up, sweet child of mine," Mom said. "We are in a massive hurry."

As I pulled the door shut, she threw the bug into gear and gunned out of the lot. A few sharp turns, and we were shooting around the back of the school and into the valley towards downtown.

"Gymnastics is the other way. And aren't you driving kind of fast?"

"Thanks for the directions, Christopher Columbus. But you're not going to class." Mom's eyes kept darting to the rear-view mirror as she swerved past slower cars.

"Excellent!" I couldn't hide my joy; I hated wearing spandex. "I mean, I'm not?"

"Nope." There was something new in her face that showed in the crease of her brow and the grim flat line of her lips: fear.

"What's wrong?"

Without explaining, she said, "Hold tight," stood on the brakes, and cranked the wheel hard left. The tyres shrieked and skidded, and the world outside the window whirled as the car spun around 180 degrees. I thought I was going to throw up.

Now we were facing the other direction. On a one-way street.

"That move," she explained, accelerating straight into oncoming traffic, "is called a bootlegger. One day I'll show you how to do it."

"Mom!" I shouted. "What are you doing?"

"Trying to lose our tail," she said, biting her lower lip and leaning forward. She jockeyed the gearshift and swung the car around a honking dump truck. Directly behind it were two dark red SUVs barrelling down on us, one in each lane.

"And this," Mom said, stomping on the gas and driving straight at them, "is called chicken."

At the last minute, the two SUVs swerved up on the pavement and thundered past on either side. I looked out of the back window and saw them both turn around.

"Why are they chasing you?" I asked.

"Us," she said, squeezing my arm. "They're after *us*. And they're chasing us because they want to capture and probably kill us, honey. But I'm not going to let them."

"Come on, Mom." I laughed like this was a bad joke. "They want to *kill* us?" When she gave me a quick look, I saw she was serious.

She blew through a red light – more honking, more squealing of brakes – and made a hard left into the entrance of Brickman Nature Preserve, where she'd enrolled me in a competitive tree-climbing class last fall. She zoomed along the scenic drive that wound uphill through the shadowy groves, leaning forward over the wheel.

"This street dead-ends at the top," I reminded her.

Behind us I caught a flash of sunlight off a windscreen —
one of the red SUVs coming after us.

Once we reached the tiny parking area at the summit,
Mom pulled up to the kerb and threw the VW into
neutral. She left the engine idling. Below us stretched the
rolling green hillside, and far off in the hazy distance,
the cluster of buildings that was downtown Stanhope,
Connecticut, the city we've called home since Brooklyn.

The park was crowded with bikers and people
walking dogs and little kids playing. A long flight of
cement steps went straight down the middle of the
grassy hill to another car park and a little lake, the water
a silvery glint barely visible past the trees.

Through the VW's open windows we could hear
engines gunning up the hill behind us — the SUVs.
Whoever they were, they were still on our tail. There
was only one exit: the road we'd taken here.

We were trapped.

"Will you tell me now what's going on?" I asked,
reaching for the door handle.

"We're taking the stairs. You're going to want to hold
on, honey." She stomped on the gas.

I hollered as we caught air off the top landing. The
engine revved hard as the wheels left the tarmac, and

I felt myself rise off the seat against the shoulder belt, saw a V of birds beat their wings against the bright blue sky—

And then the car crashed down on to the steps.

The doors caught on the banisters and the side-view mirrors popped off. The air bags blew out and slammed me back against the seat.

Somehow my mom kept driving.

The car was a tight fit between the railings, but not so tight that we got stuck. Reaching around the air bag, Mom kept working the gearshift and the gas, and the bug bolted forward, bouncing and rattling and banging as it hit every one of the steps.

At the landing halfway down, we slowed. The air bags had deflated a bit, but now everything in the car — including me and my mom — was covered with a powdery grey dust that stank like new rubber. "Are you crazy?" I asked, coughing. "Can we just stop and talk—"

But we were off again. With an enormous scrape, we began jouncing down the second long flight.

All this time, my mom was jabbing at the horn — as though anyone could miss the car screeching its way down the steps. Through the windscreen I watched people dive over the banisters, screaming as they ran.

At last, with a teeth-snapping bang, we reached the foot of the stairs and Mom brought the car to a stop. "Are you OK, honey?" she asked, reaching over and patting my shoulder and face. "Talk to me, Ronan."

"I'm fine," I said. I wiped my face clean with my hoodie, then leaned out of the window. The sides of the bug were crumpled, and steam was billowing out from beneath the hood. The engine made little ticking sounds as a puddle of liquid slowly spread out from under the engine. "Mom, what are you doing?" I asked. "We could have just *died*."

But her head was turned away. She was staring in the other direction, back the way we'd come.

At the top of the hill, stark against the bright sky, one of the red SUVs had tried the same stunt we'd just pulled but had been pinned by the railings. The other SUV was parked alongside, its grill flush against the railing. Five men and a woman, all wearing dark blue suits, stood watching from above.

"Who are those people?" I asked.

"Bad guys," my mom said. "It's complicated." Her voice sounded remarkably calm, but when she put the car back into gear, her hand shook. "Someone trashed the house – looking for something – and now your dad has . . . gone missing."

That was the final straw, the thing that finally convinced me my mom was delusional. She announces we're being pursued by people who want to kill us. *Sure.* She risks our lives and trashes the VW. *OK.* But the news that my father – nerdy, quiet, absent Dad, who is the comptroller (whatever that means) for a multinational conglomerate (whatever that is) has been kidnapped? *No way.*

"Why would anyone want to kidnap Dad?" I asked. "He's like a fancy accountant."

She didn't reply. In silence we tooled along the broad cement walkway that ran by the lake, following its gentle curves towards the car park on the far side.

"Maybe it was *him*," I insisted. "Maybe he was looking for something, and he was just sloppy. Did you think of that?"

"*Yes,* I thought of that, Ronan," Mom snapped, using her discussion-is-over voice. "There are a couple of things you should know," she said, honking at a redhead woman pushing a stroller. The woman steered it off the path in a hurry. "First, the truth about me. I'm part of a group called the Blood Guard. We protect people from bad guys." She exhaled sharply. "That's the important thing. I'm one of the good guys, Ronan. And so are you."

"Blood Guard?" I repeated. "Does Dad know about this?"

I was thrown hard against my seat belt as Mom punched the brakes. The car squealed to a stop. "Maybe," she said with a sigh. "Maybe he knows."

We'd reached a little parking area. It was empty — except for the police car parked sideways across the exit, the lights on its roof spinning blue and red. Crouched down outside the car, behind the front end, were a man and a woman.

They had their pistols drawn. Aimed straight at us.

Mom reached behind me and rooted around. When she came forward again, she was holding something long, curved and dark — a sword in a fancy leather scabbard.

"What's that?" I asked, even though I knew; I'd been taking fencing classes since fourth grade. In the back seat was a large open duffel bag full of swords and other dangerous-looking things. And a blue suitcase. *My* blue suitcase.

"Cutlass," she said, closing her eyes and whispering a few words under her breath.

"Mom, those are *cops*. They have *guns*."

My mom rested her hand on my arm. "Those aren't real police officers, Ronan."

They looked real enough to me. It *was* a little strange that they weren't wearing uniforms. Or caps. I couldn't see them too well behind the car, but the woman had inky black hair, and the guy was bald.

"The second thing," Mom said, her teeth gritted in anger, "is that people are often not who they pretend to be. They lie. Those two out there?" She nodded towards the police car, pushed her door open and slid the cutlass from its scabbard. It came loose with a pretty metallic chime. "They're killers. If you're going to survive, Ronan, you'll have to heed my warning: *trust no one.*"

"Sure thing," I said, thinking maybe I shouldn't trust *her.*

"Stay in the car and keep down, honey. There may be ricochets."

And just like that Mom was galloping across the car park, swinging the cutlass.

CHAPTER TWO

THE MOST DANGEROUS
MOM ALIVE

She ran straight at the police car.

The blade she carried gleamed bright blue, like it had stored up the light of a full moon. Every sweep of its point left a bright, burning arc in the air.

But that wasn't what made my jaw drop with wonder.

When my mom ran, she *blurred*. There was a moment when her legs were visible; then something shifted, and she was a smear of colour streaking across the tarmac, halving the distance between us and the police car in a single breath. No regular person moves that fast.

But she still wasn't fast enough: before she reached the two cops, I saw light flare from the muzzles of their pistols.

The gunfire didn't faze my mom at all.

There was a shimmery halo of silver around her as she spun her cutlass, followed by an ear-stinging series of clangs. And then she soared into the air with a jump that carried her forty feet in a heartbeat.

Midair, she tucked and somersaulted. When she came out of the roll, she swept out her right leg and caught the bald guy hard on the side of his head. He went down as she landed lightly in a crouch on the hood of the car, the point of her sword poised against the woman's neck.

The woman dropped her gun and raised her hands.

I scrambled out of the VW. By the time I reached them, my mom had cuffed the woman and her unconscious partner to the rusted metal gate of the car park.

"You will burn!" the woman snarled through clenched teeth.

My mom went through the unconscious man's pockets.

Up close, the woman and her partner definitely didn't look like police officers. They wore dark suits, like Secret Service agents, and on the wrists of their cuffed left hands were two identical tattoos: a wide-open eye.

"Nice tat," I said.

My mom's head snapped up. "Ronan! I *told* you to stay in the car. You need to *listen* when I tell you something."

The woman thrashed on the ground, scrambling to reach two long swords in woven cloth scabbards that lay on the tarmac by the car. My mother kicked the weapons aside, and the woman spat at her. "You will burn!"

"So you keep saying." My mom turned back to me. "Ronan, get our bags."

I ran to the VW, slung my backpack over my shoulder, grabbed my suitcase and the duffel full of weapons, then rushed back across the car park.

Mom tossed our luggage into the back of the police car, then threw her own car keys deep into the shade of the trees. We climbed in. "See if you can figure out how to get the siren going."

"Seriously, now you're stealing a police car?" I asked. "What the hell is going on?"

Mom smiled and pushed my hair out of my face, then eased the car towards the exit. "Ronan, honey, do me a favour and buckle up, would you? Also, don't use the word *hell*. It's not polite language for a young man."

Running the siren really made people pay attention.

Cars careened wildly to the side of the road when they

heard us coming and stayed out of the way until we'd passed. Mom rarely dropped below sixty as she took us out of the park, over the river and into downtown Stanhope.

It all might have been fun if a bunch of people hadn't just tried to kill us.

Any doubts I'd had before vanished when I'd watched my mom take down those two fake cops in the park. I studied her face as she drove, searching for . . . I don't know what. Some hint that my mother had *always* led a secret life in which she stole police cars and took down gun-toting bad guys with ease and belonged to a secret society called the Blood Guard.

But all I could see was my regular old mom.

She squinted into the rear-view mirror. "Rats."

"What is it?"

"They figured out we switched cars." She spun the wheel, and with a squeal, the police car turned a perfect ninety degrees into an alleyway between two looming skyscrapers. We bounced through one alley, then another, and suddenly we were on a sleepy downtown street lined with glass-fronted buildings. A few people strolled along the pavement.

"Is Dad – is he going to be OK?" It wasn't fair.

My dad was completely harmless. He was one of those guys who never looked comfortable except when he was in a suit. He wore dorky glasses and an even dorkier beard that he'd grown when he started going bald. He worked hard – so hard that he'd all but disappeared into his job the past couple of years. After we'd moved to Connecticut, I'd barely seen him at all.

"They won't hurt him, honey – not before I track them down and put an end to this business."

"I'll go with you!" I said. "I can handle a sword. Remember? You made me take fencing lessons!" And suddenly the years of extracurricular activities made sense. Mom had always said all those classes were for self-improvement, or to "round me out" and help me get into a good college. But really she'd been training me, preparing me for a day like this one.

Mom smiled. "Unfortunately, you can't help with this, Ronan. It's something I have to do alone, and I can only do that if I know you're safe. That's why I'm taking you to the train station." She turned down a side street and sped down a trash-strewn alley, before finally pulling into an underground parking garage.

In the moment it took my eyes to adjust to the cool

shadows, Mom had rolled us around the ramp and into a dark corner.

"You'll find a ticket in the top pocket of your suitcase for the three forty-one to Washington, DC. Make sure you're on that train – that's where your escort expects to find you."

"Escort?" Everything was moving way too fast. "Who?"

She bit her lip. "Someone from the Guard. There wasn't time to find out exactly who." She gently shook my left shoulder. "This is important: your escort will tell you the time if you ask."

"The *time*? Mom, *anyone* will tell me the time if I ask politely enough."

"But your escort will tell you it's twelve minutes till midnight." She pointed to the door of a stairwell, dimly visible in the gloom. "From the top of those stairs it's only a couple of blocks to the station. Don't dawdle."

"You're just dumping me here?"

Taking my face in her hands, she stared into my eyes, and I saw she was scared – maybe not of the people chasing us, but of sending me away by myself. "Someone has to lead them away from you, and that someone has to be me. I'll be in touch soon, I promise." She pulled me forward into a crushing hug. "I don't tell you this enough, but I really do love you, Ronan."

Tears stung my eyes, and for a moment I thought she wasn't going to let go. Then she pushed me back, dragged the back of her hand across her nose and said, "Now get out and do as I said."

"Wait—"

"There is no time for *wait*, Ronan. You need to be on that train."

When I still didn't move, she said, "Honey. Please."

So I slung my backpack and my suitcase out of the car, pulled up the suitcase handle and rolled it over to the stairwell. I looked back from the doorway and my mother smiled at me. I could see the shiny tracks of her tears even in the dim light of the garage. Then she gave the engine some gas and quietly drove out of the parking garage.

That's when I knew this was all for real, and there was a good chance I might never see my mother or father again.

CHAPTER THREE

I TAKE A BATHROOM BREAK

It was two short blocks to the train station. Striding along the pavements were lots of business people, moms with kids and old people who just seemed to be out enjoying the nice weather. The world seemed totally normal.

Until, when I was across the street from the station, a red SUV zoomed past.

I froze, and someone ploughed into me from behind.

"Sorry about that, old boy," the guy said. He was young – eighteen, maybe – and so wire-hanger skinny that his brown leather jacket hung slack from his shoulders and his belt barely held up his black jeans. Under his jacket was a dirty red T-shirt with a drawing of a very tired-looking cat hugging an enormous coffee mug, and the words I'LL SLEEP WHEN I'M DEAD.

He pushed his shaggy blond hair behind his ears, smiled briefly at me and said, "Best get moving – you don't want to be late for your train!" And then he ambled through the intersection and disappeared through the station doors.

I took a deep breath, crossed the street myself and followed him inside.

The Grand Terminus in Stanhope is like a lot of train stations on the East Coast: huge and imposing and kind of run-down.

Giant pillars support the roof several storeys overhead, and huge arched windows let in a dusty grey light that makes the polished marble tile floor look slick, like something in a king's palace. You can tell that, once upon a time, trains were a big honking deal, but now these stations stink of dust and varnish, and the wooden benches look old and uncomfortable, and the low hum of noise within the walls sounds like the echoes of all the people who've passed through. It can be kind of creepy, especially if you're feeling creeped out already.

Which I completely was.

I hauled my suitcase over to one of the benches and sat down, rooting around in its front pocket for my ticket. My mom wasn't kidding: I found a one-way to DC and a creamy envelope with her handwriting on the outside: *Give this to your Guard escort. BE CAREFUL WITH IT. It's very valuable. I love you, Mom.* It bulged with something heavy. When I opened it up, a purplish glass disc about as big and thick as a cracker slid out into my palm. A twisty, tarnished silver frame covered its edges, and there was a little loop of metal on one side. It looked like an antique monocle.

I held it up to my eye: through the violet lens, people became dark shadows, and the light rippled like oil on water, but that was all. I looked at the giant old-fashioned clock over the ticket desk: 3:27. Fourteen minutes until my train departed. I slid the lens back into the envelope and put it and the ticket into a pocket of my jeans.

I slid my phone out of my backpack and turned it on, and it immediately started buzzing like crazy with all the missed calls and texts my mom had sent while I was in school. There were a dozen texts, each more alarming than the last. Things like:

CALL ME AS SOON AS YOU GET THIS!

and

DON'T GO HOME! THIS IS VERY IMPORTANT!!!

and finally, the one that spooked me the most:

TRUST NO ONE.

I was so freaked out by the messages that I almost missed the woman.

Even across the vast waiting area, it was clear that she was staring straight at me. And me alone. She was tall and blonde and looked like she worked in an office, prim and proper in a dark suit and a crisp white shirt and slick black loafers – what my mom always referred to as "sensible shoes". There was something about her that made my flesh crawl, though it took me a moment to realize what it was: she never looked away. It was hard to tell from this distance, but I was pretty sure she never even blinked.

Weird.

I stood up and pretended to look at the giant departure board high on the wall. She raised a phone to her ear.

Of course, she wasn't alone.

Over by the long marble ticket counter, two men in identical blue suits started marching stiffly towards me. On the other side of the room, from the archway that led to the platforms, two other blue suits appeared. Then a fifth guy came in off the street.

The six of them casually closed in on my bench, as though they all just happened to be strolling in my direction.

Panic squeezed my chest. My mom had trusted me to get on the train, and I couldn't even get out of the station waiting room.

No way could I run past them to the train platforms, or make a break for the street, or even reach the guard at the far end of the ticket counter. "Sorry, Mom," I whispered.

The five guys stopped about twenty feet away, forming a loose semicircle and closing off any hope of escape. The blonde woman, who was clearly the boss, walked straight towards me. "Evelyn Ronan Truelove," she said, "there is nowhere to run."

But she was wrong. I turned and sprinted for the only place she couldn't follow.

I wrestled my suitcase through the door of the men's room. It looked mostly empty. An old man stood at the long row of grimy sinks, washing his hands. A guy in a janitor's uniform was in the corner, wearily leaning on a mop. I rolled past them and peered around the corner, hoping to find another exit.

There wasn't one. Just an overflowing trash can against the wall, and eight ancient green toilet stalls along a wall of windows that looked like they hadn't been cleaned since the year I was born. All of the stalls were in use.

Or almost all. I dragged my suitcase into the third, slid the bolt home and sat down. The back of the door was covered with graffiti, years of scribbles like cave drawings. On top of everything, someone had written DONT LOOK BACK!!! in silver paint. *Needs an apostrophe*, I thought.

The blonde woman couldn't come into the men's room, but her five henchmen sure could. Would they really apprehend a kid in a toilet stall while Mop Man watched? Not likely. So they would probably just guard the exit and make sure I missed my train.

All they had to do was wait me out. I couldn't sit on a toilet for ever.

Except they weren't interested in being patient.

The bathroom door banged open, followed by the sharp clack of footsteps – hard heels against tile. I carefully pulled my suitcase away from the stall door and tried not to hyperventilate.

A pair of pointy black leather shoes paced slowly past the door. At the far end of the line of stalls, I heard a rap of knuckles. A man bellowed, "I'm busy in here!" A few more slow footsteps, another knock, and then another man's voice saying, "*Ocupado!*"

I glanced at my phone. My train left in four minutes. I had to get out of here.

I stared at the back of the stall door. DONT LOOK BACK!!!

Why not? The window behind the toilet was made of big double panes of frosted glass and had no lock. I quietly twisted the latch and raised the pane as far as it would go. A fresh breeze blew in, and I could see outside the bathroom into some sort of access way for station workers.

The space was wide enough for me to slide through, but getting out wasn't going to be easy. Even standing on the toilet seat, the window sill was at shoulder height — scrambling up there was going to be a noisy business.

I dangled my backpack through the window and let it drop.

There was a knock on the stall door next to mine. Instead of answering, the man in there flushed his toilet.

Praying the sound was loud enough to mask the noise of my escape, I closed my eyes and thought of gymnastics.

I know, I know – I'm trapped in a public toilet, a bunch of mysterious people after me and my parents fighting for their lives somewhere else. Leotards and ten-point landings and bendy moves on the parallel bars should be the furthest thing from my mind.

But my training took over – I just needed to put my weight on my hands and throw myself forward in a vault. If only I weren't starting in an awkward standing position with my feet on the rim of a toilet. There was no way I'd be able to jerk myself up sharply enough—

There was a rap on my stall door.

I took a deep breath, visualized the move. . .

And just like that, I was soaring head first up and out. I arced over the sill and landed gently on my feet in the access way.

"Never done *that* before," I whispered, wishing my coach had been around to see.

Through the window behind me, I heard another knock.

"Evelyn," the man said, his voice flat, like he was

imitating a robot. "I know you're there. Come out. We're here to help."

I grabbed the sill and pulled my head back up level with the window. And saw my suitcase. I'd totally forgotten it. "Just a minute!" I shouted. "Also, can you do me a favour? Like, seriously – don't call me Evelyn."

And then something occurred to me. Maybe I had it all wrong and *these* people were the good guys. Maybe they were the ones I was supposed to meet. I cleared my throat. "Hey, do you know what time it is?"

No answer.

After a moment, the door rattled and the man said, "It is *time* for you to open this door, Evelyn. No need to make a scene. We have important information for you. About your father."

Not the good guys, then.

Only two minutes until my train left. No chance I'd be able to get the suitcase. Good thing I had the ticket in my pocket.

The guy banged on the stall door hard enough that it shook on its hinges. "You will come out, and you will come out now. Or we will drag you out."

Someone in the bathroom hollered, "Let the boy do his business. I'm calling security!"

I'd heard enough. I dropped back to the ground, looped my hand through my backpack and ran full tilt down the path to the platform.

The train was one of those slick new ones like a spaceship inside, all white plastic walls and glass doors between cars that hush open when you press a button. I tried to look like I belonged before finally plopping down on to an empty royal blue seat that faced the back of the train. I wanted to be able to see anyone coming after me.

I took a deep, shuddery breath. My phone read 3:40.

All sorts of people boarded at the last minute, stumbling with their bags and looking for seats, but the blonde woman from the station never turned up, and neither did her five pals.

At last the doors of the train hissed shut. An automated voice came over the intercom to announce our on-time departure and the train slowly began to move.

I hadn't realized how tense I was until I felt myself relax.

I gazed out at the platform rolling past the window and tried to calm my heartbeat. I was safe. I had got away. Sure, I had lost the suitcase my mom had packed, and I only had twelve dollars in my wallet, but I still had my phone and my backpack and my train ticket. DC was three hours away; I'd find whoever I was supposed to meet and then I'd get some answers.

Then I noticed one of the blue-suited guys loping along the platform, easily keeping pace. He must have been running hard, but his black hair stayed perfectly combed and parted, his face blank.

He ran up to one of the train windows, peered inside, then put on a burst of speed until he reached the next. One window after another, he drew closer and closer to where I was sitting.

There was something freakily unreal about the machinelike way his arms moved up and down like pistons as he ran. He wasn't even breaking a sweat.

And then he saw me.

His eyes narrowed and he swerved my way. When he was just outside the window, he brought his hand back, made a fist, and swung it like a hammer at the glass.

The noise was so loud I flinched. A spider's web of faint cracks appeared in the centre of the pane.

Across the aisle, a kid said, "Cool!"

"Someone call the conductor!" said the kid's mom.

The blue-suited man pulled his fist back for another blow.

But he wasn't looking where he was going, and as he swung at the window again, the platform ended. He plunged out of sight without a sound.

I sat back and took one deep breath after another, until my pulse stopped thudding in my ears.

That was what my mom was up against. Alone. And where was I? Safe on a train. I should have been with her, helping rescue my dad. Somewhere out there she was driving around town in a stolen police car, a bagful of swords at her side, creeps like the blonde woman and her friends in hot pursuit. And worse, my dad was who knows where, worrying that these people, whoever they were, were going to kill him.

I stared at the spot where the guy in the suit had disappeared. "I hope that hurt," I whispered.

CHAPTER FOUR

YOU'VE GOT TO PICK A POCKET OR TWO

I emptied my busted old yellow backpack on to the seat beside me.

There wasn't a single thing that was going to be useful if those people caught up to me. A massive hardbound textbook. A novel called *Fahrenheit 451* that we were reading for English. A bunch of pens and a binder full of class notes that I'd never bothered to look at. And, wadded up at the bottom, my embarrassing gymnastics outfit – like *that* would come in handy if I needed a change of clothes.

I checked my phone for a message from my mom, but there was nothing new. So I did something stupid: I called my dad's mobile.

I don't know what I was thinking. That my dad would answer, maybe, and tell me that this was all a mistake, that my mother was confused, that he wasn't in trouble. That he'd laugh and tell me everything was OK.

Someone picked up on the third ring. "Evelyn," said a man who wasn't my dad. "Where are you right now?"

I hung up. Almost immediately the phone buzzed in my hand: whoever it was, calling back. In a panic, I powered down the phone and shoved it and everything else inside my backpack, then stashed it in the overhead luggage rack.

That's when I saw him – the skinny older kid who'd bumped into me outside the station. He was doing a Good Samaritan thing now, helping two white-haired ladies with their enormous bags.

As I watched, wondering what grandmas pack that takes up so much space – knitting? extra cats? every warm blanket ever created? – I saw the skinny guy slide something from the front pocket of one of the bags and slip it into his jacket.

A ticket. He'd stolen one of the ladies' train tickets.

With the suitcases stowed away, the skinny guy bowed. The old women thanked him, and he sauntered down the aisle into the next car.

I didn't pause to think; I went after him. Maybe I couldn't help my mom or dad, but I could at least take care of this thief. I'd make him give the ticket back, have him thrown off the train.

The glass door between the cars hissed open and I worked my way forward, glancing at the passengers.

At the end of the car, I nearly tripped over his feet. He'd reclined across an entire row, his scarecrow legs in their black jeans stretched out in front of him, his scuffed old Doc Martens hanging in the aisle. He was slouched against the window, engrossed in a cheap yellow spiral-bound notebook, doodling.

"You!" I said, pointing. I hadn't really thought about what I'd say after that.

"Yup, me," he said, lifting an eyebrow as he stashed the notebook inside his brown leather jacket. "Did you want to know the time?" He had a ghost of an accent, a faint British lilt.

"I saw you steal that woman's ticket."

"Ach, she doesn't need it. Not really. But you know who does? *Me*."

"Of course she needs it!" Didn't she? "Anyway, she bought it."

"Have a seat." He folded his legs under him and gestured. "I don't really like that whole you-standing-over-me thing. Puts a crick in my neck having to look up at you."

I didn't know what else to do, so I sat down next to him. He smelled a little bit, like he hadn't showered in a few days. "I'm going to tell the conductor," I said. "He'll have you thrown off the train."

"Is that really what you want?" He drew his dirty blond hair behind his ears, scratched the stubble along his chin and said, "Look, where's the harm in it? No one is going to give an old lady a hard time for losing her ticket – most people just aren't bred that mean. They'll think she mislaid it and they'll give her a pass. Meantime, I helped her with her bags, and—"

"Tickets, please."

I hadn't even noticed the approach of the conductor. Without thinking, I found myself passing my ticket over. The man punched it, gave it back, then slid a green tag into the shelf edge over my head.

"Is it long to Washington?" the thief asked, handing over his – I mean, the old lady's – ticket.

"Oh, just a bit over three hours. Time enough for two teenage boys to get into trouble." The conductor's smile beneath his grey, bushy moustache appeared kind. "Mind that you don't."

"Yes, sir," said the thief.

And then the conductor moved on.

"I was just an accomplice to a crime," I muttered. I was completely useless unless someone like my mom was telling me what to do. No wonder she got me out of the way.

"Don't worry yourself," said the thief. "I'm fine, you're fine, the old biddies will be fine. It's survival of the fleetest."

"Fittest," I said. "The phrase is 'survival of the fittest'."

"You've got a lot to learn, Evelyn Ronan Truelove." The thief extended one of his grimy hands. "Jack Dawkins, at your service."

My heart hammered. Everything my mom had done to get me safe, everything I'd gone through, and I'm so stupid that I sat down right beside—

"Don't go getting all pale around the gills," Dawkins said. "You didn't ask me *the time*. You were supposed to ask so that I could tell you it is twelve minutes to midnight."

I collapsed against the seat. "Why didn't you *say* something when you saw me outside?"

"Didn't know for sure what we'd find in that station." He shrugged and looked thoughtful. "Makes no sense they'd be after you. But something very strange is going on."

"After *me*," I repeated.

"Yes, but don't worry – if they'd taken you before you got on the train, I'd have swooped in and saved the day." His face broke into another bright smile and I found myself smiling back.

"They almost caught me in the bathroom."

"No kidding!" He laughed. "Who do you think it was shouting about security? And may I say, well done slipping out of the bathroom window like that. I don't know how you managed, but it threw that bunch into a panic."

"Thanks." For the first time all day, I felt a tiny bit proud of myself.

There was a sudden noise, like an animal howling from underneath the seat.

I clutched the armrest. "What was that?"

"My stomach, Ronan. That's how it tells me it's hungry." He stood up and shooed me forward. "Come on. There's got to be a café somewhere on this lousy conveyance."

As he led the way down the aisle, the train rocked – a tiny jostle, not all that big a deal – but somehow it sent Dawkins sprawling face-first into the midst of a family on holiday. He practically fell upon the father, who helped set him back on his feet.

"Sorry!" Dawkins said, straightening the man's coat.

At the far end of the car, Dawkins rotated his hand and revealed a sleek black wallet he'd lifted from the man's jacket. Fishing out a wad of twenties, he dropped the wallet into the trash slot and said, "Onward! I've got an emptiness within me that no number of hot dogs will be able to fill."

A few minutes later, Dawkins ordered what he called "a snack": eight hot dogs, as many hamburgers, five chocolate bars, two huge plates of gooey nachos, a couple of bags of crisps and six diet sodas. "I'm watching my weight," he said with a wink.

The dining car was lined with blue vinyl bench seats facing each other across white Formica tables, and there was a tiny snack bar in the middle manned by an older woman with bleached blonde hair. Her name tag read

BRENDA. "All that food, just for you?" she asked. "I'm going to have to get you a bigger tray!"

She produced a turquoise fibreglass tray from a cupboard, and Dawkins mounded everything on to it. He sat down in the first booth and I slid into the bench opposite.

"What is this Blood Guard thing?" I asked. "And who were those people in the station?"

"All in good time." He fluffed out a napkin and tucked it into the neck of his T-shirt. He wasn't as young as I'd first thought. He *looked* like he was a senior in high school, but something about his eyes seemed – there's no other word for it – *old*. "In the Guard, it pays to eat fast, before some nasty sort tries to stick a knife in you."

Dawkins began folding the hot dogs in half in their buns and shoving them into his mouth. He'd chew vigorously for a moment, take a mouthful of soda, then swallow with an audible *gulp*. He shoved the last hot dog my way, saying, "You should eat something."

I shook my head *no*, feeling queasy.

"Your call, old boy." He leaned back, placed his hands on his belly and belched. "OK, then. To understand the Blood Guard, you need to understand who it is they protect. Among the seven billion or so people on this planet, there exist thirty-six who are better than all the rest of us put together. Thirty-six pure souls. Deep down, these people are genuinely *good* – so much so that they make up for the darkness and sins committed by the other six billion and something people on Earth." He worked something out of his teeth with his tongue. "They're not a bunch of goody two-shoes. It's more that they radiate a kind of . . . purity of spirit, let's call it."

"Sure," I said. "Thirty-six awesome people somewhere in the world."

He shook his head. "Not *somewhere*, not all together like some classroom full of A-plus students. No, just scattered around the planet, like diamonds in a dump truck full of pebbles." He noisily slurped one of his sodas. "You with me so far?"

"Thirty-six diamonds in a bunch of pebbles." I listened for a moment to the train's wheels clattering against the track. "But what does this have to do with my dad being kidnapped? Or my mom being. . ." I didn't know what to call her. *Badass?*

"I'm getting there." He tore open a bag of crisps and emptied half of them into his mouth. "The thirty-six appear in many mystical writings as the Righteous Ones, or the *Tzadikim Nistarim*, or simply the Pure.

"The sources all agree on one point," Dawkins continued. "The Pure are the only thing that stops God from saying, 'Enough already!' wiping the world clean and starting over." He cleaned his mouth with a wadded-up napkin. "Noah's flood happened because there were too few Pure in the world. Whenever even *one* of the Pure dies, the entire world suffers."

"You believe that God is going to destroy the world if thirty-six people aren't here?" My mom might not have been crazy, but this guy was obviously bonkers.

"Think of it like the spokes on a bicycle wheel. Snap one and the wheel still holds its shape, right? Take out three spokes and it starts to warp. Seven and the warping gets pretty bad. You don't have to remove every spoke to make the wheel collapse. The Second World War happened because five of the Pure had been found and murdered. The Dark Ages? Eight Pure had been killed, and as a result, the world was plunged into centuries of misery, ignorance and plague."

"But these thirty-six people have to die sometime," I said. "No one lives for ever."

"That's what you'd think," Dawkins said with a smirk. "A natural death isn't the problem; a Pure's soul is reincarnated almost instantaneously. It's when the Pure dies before his *appointed* time – when that Pure is murdered – that the world suffers during the long wait for the soul to come back into being."

Brenda came around from behind the snack bar and walked over. "Just put the tray back when you're done," she told him. "I'm going to take my break."

He gave her a thumbs-up, and the dining car was empty except for us.

Dawkins licked his fingers. "Anyway, as I was saying, the Pure are vitally important. Which is where the Blood Guard comes in. The Guard was brought into being to protect the Pure, because they can't protect themselves."

"Why not? Are they super wimpy or something?"

"Because they don't know what they are."

"Couldn't you just gather them all together and hide them in a castle or something?"

"The Pure can't know *what* they are or it changes *who* they are. See, part of what makes them so special is that they don't have any skin in the game. You know how ugly some very pretty people can become once they've *learned* they're pretty? It's like that. When one of the thirty-six learns he is pure, he loses that essential goodness and stops being pure. And, as a result, the world becomes a tiny bit darker, steps a tiny bit closer to ruin.

"So we can't really tell them anything, and we can't let anyone know who they are. No one knows their identity — no one but the members of the Blood Guard. The Guard does its work in secret, living a regular life while watching over and protecting the Pure."

"I don't understand what this has to do with my mom and dad," I said.

"Your mum is one of the Blood Guard," Dawkins said. "Her identity was blown and your home was ransacked — in a search for clues about the identity of the Pure she was guarding."

"And my dad was kidnapped," I said. "To put pressure on my mom? To get her to reveal this Pure person?"

"That makes sense," he said, shuffling the food around on his tray.

"So why are they chasing me?" I asked.

"That's the big mystery," Dawkins replied. "Our enemies are up to something, and it involves you. That's all I know."

"So what's the plan?" I asked. "You take me to DC and we meet my mom there?"

After a quick swallow of soda, he said, "I'll hand you

over to another Guard in DC and then I'll go find your mum. You'll be safe with Ogabe." He began peeling the wrappers away from his chocolate bars like they were bananas.

Outside the window, the landscape had gone from city grey to woodsy green. Connecticut and New York were behind us. The seat rocked gently beneath me and everything seemed weirdly peaceful. I thought about the man slamming his fist against the window, but that seemed almost unreal now. "I don't really believe all this," I said.

"Believe what you like, Ronan Truelove," said Dawkins. "Your faith doesn't matter one way or another. I'm just telling you like it is." He started in on the nachos.

"So is stealing from old grannies part of being in the Blood Guard?"

A Snickers bar disappeared in two sharp bites. "A Guard has to move with stealth, and sometimes, yes, even petty thievery." He waggled his thin eyebrows. "I move like a shadow on the world, leaving no trace."

He winked.

And then, "Thieves!" a girl's voice cried out.

She stood in the doorway; about my age, skinny and almost freakishly pale, with long red hair pulled up on top of her head in some kind of elastic thingy and held in place by a whole bunch of beaded hairpins and barrettes. She was dressed in jeans and a green sleeveless top, nothing too fancy. She might even have been beautiful except that her expression was so angry it was hard to tell.

I recognized her right away.

She pointed at Dawkins. "You stole that man's wallet when you fell on him. I *saw* you!"

"Move like a shadow on the world?" I muttered. "*Sure.*"

But Dawkins wasn't paying me any attention. Instead, he was staring at the girl while he chewed a hamburger, clearly alarmed. "You really should butt out and go back to your seat," he told her.

"The conductor is searching for the two of you right now, and when he finds you, he's going to lock you up," she said, gaining confidence as she saw how upset Dawkins was. "Maybe he'll handcuff you to a seat or something. Or maybe they'll just stop the train and have the police take you away."

"Greta Sustermann," I said, deciding it was time to speak up.

Greta was probably the smartest person in my old

school, back in Brooklyn.

"Ronan Truelove?" Greta said, her brow furrowing. "Loser loner arsonist?"

Sometimes also the most annoying.

"I did not set my house on fire!" I protested. "And you were in the same honours classes with me, so if I'm a loser, so are you."

"Is that why you left school? To ride the rails with" – she sniffed loudly – "really filthy pickpockets?"

"'Ride the rails'?" I repeated. "Who even talks like that?"

"You *know* this girl?" Dawkins wiped his mouth with a napkin and slid to the edge of the booth. "No one is going to jail, missy."

"I'm not a *missy*, you creep," Greta said, reaching into a boxy blue purse that was slung over her shoulder and taking out a slim little smartphone.

"My name," Dawkins said, "is Jack Dawkins. What are you doing there?"

"Texting my *dad*, who happens to be in law enforcement, to see what *he* advises the conductor to do. You are going to answer for your crimes, sir."

"I really wish you wouldn't do that," Dawkins said.

"And I really wish you weren't a scummy thief,"

Greta said, her fingers flying across the touch pad. "It's only a matter of time before your crimes catch up with you."

"That time has already come," Dawkins said, frowning. He popped the last bite of Butterfinger into his mouth, then stood and waved. "Hello there!"

A man in a blue suit had come in so silently that I hadn't even noticed. He passed soundlessly within inches of Greta, ignoring her completely. He was a different guy from the one who'd run alongside the train – for one thing, this guy's hair was thin and completely colourless, like it was spun from dental floss – but he was dressed exactly the same: natty blue suit over a white shirt.

"Greta," Dawkins said, picking up the turquoise tray and backing up. Floss Hair followed him towards the centre of the car. "Be a good sport and take a seat in the booth with Ronan."

There was a faint *whoosh* from the other end of the car, beyond the snack bar, and I saw that Floss Hair hadn't come alone.

Another blue suit had appeared. Like Floss Hair, he was quiet and impassive, but this guy was as bald as Mr Clean. And also like Floss Hair, he was wielding something long, shiny and sharp, with a fine silvery edge that caught the light.

Greta sat down hard across from me, her phone forgotten in her hand. "What are they holding. . . ?" she asked.

"Swords," I answered.

CHAPTER FIVE

PUSH COMES TO SHOVE

"Spadroons, to be specific," Dawkins corrected. "Not to be technical and all, but accuracy is always nice." He glanced over his shoulder at the bald man advancing his way. "Two against one?" he said to Floss Hair. "That's hardly sporting."

Floss Hair didn't answer, just levelled his weapon.

"But *why* do they have swords?" Greta asked. "Isn't that overkill for a couple of ticket thieves?"

"We're not ticket th—" I started, then corrected myself. "OK, maybe Dawkins is, but I'm not. Anyway, those guys have nothing to do with that."

"So who are they?"

I shrugged. "They're . . . bad guys, I guess."

"You *guess?*" she said. "Did the swords clue you in?"

"Here's a lesson for you, Ronan," Dawkins interrupted. "A Blood Guard finds weapons in whatever he has at hand." As Floss Hair rushed him, he swept the food tray upward. With a sharp *crack*, it knocked the blade aside in a messy shower of mustard-splattered cardboard, chocolate wrappers and nacho-glooped napkins.

Floss Hair spun and slashed backwards, but Dawkins was ready for the move and used the flat of the tray like a shield to block the blade.

"Behind you," I warned. Mr Clean was half a car away but jogging forward.

"He's still out of reach," Dawkins said, glancing over his shoulder. "Plenty of time for me to—"

He parried another thrust from Floss Hair, using the tray to push the blade aside. Floss Hair tried to step back, but Dawkins was too quick: he swung the tray straight up against the man's jaw with an audible snap. Floss Hair's eyes rolled back and he slumped unconscious to the floor.

A split second later, Dawkins had the man's sword clenched in his right hand and brought it around in time to deflect the bald man's blade at his back.

Mr Clean hopped back out of range, edging alongside the snack bar.

"Now this is more like it," Dawkins said, swinging the sword in the air. With his left hand, he whipped the tray forward like a Frisbee.

It caught Mr Clean in the shin with a loud crack. It sounded like it hurt, but the man didn't say a word, just winced and fell to his knees.

"Where's your Hand?" Dawkins demanded of the man.

"What's he talking about?" Greta asked me.

"Hands, maybe?" I whispered, confused.

As if in response, the man raised his left arm, gestured at the snack bar, made a fist, then opened his palm towards Dawkins. There was a blast of wind and all the junk on the counter – napkins, coffee stirrers, salt and pepper packets, a coffee pot – flew forward.

"*Down!*" Dawkins yelled.

Greta and I dived under the table.

As I did, I glimpsed Dawkins swirling the blade around himself in a bright halo of steel, his sword arm moving blindingly fast as he carved his way through the airborne trash. None of it touched him.

With a quick *thwip-thwip-thwip*, the vinyl bench where we'd just been sitting suddenly bristled with little spikes – coffee stirrers, I realized, sunk inches deep into the cushions.

"You guys are in so much trouble," Greta whispered.

There was a sharp, piercing ring of steel on steel, an ear-splitting clash of swords.

I peeked around the corner of the booth. Dawkins and Mr Clean swung and hacked at each other, grunting and panting with every slash and thrust. Within a handful of seconds, they'd each struck and parried a dozen times.

But Dawkins was the better swordsman.

Mr Clean was hemmed in by the narrow passage between the snack bar and the wall of the dining car and couldn't really swing his spadroon.

"Ronan?" Dawkins called back over his shoulder.

I stuck my head out. "Yeah?"

"That bleach-haired bloke by the window? Search him." Floss Hair looked almost peaceful, like a businessman who had just decided to take a nap on the dining-car floor.

"You mean, like, go through his pockets?"

"Yes, Ronan – that's what *search* usually means." Dawkins lunged after Mr Clean, slashing in great sweeps, driving the bald man back.

I crawled across the carpet to Floss Hair's side, and nearly yelped when I saw Greta on her hands and knees right beside me.

"What?" she said. "I'm not staying back there alone." There was a wild glint in her eyes. "Go on. Search him."

Before I did, though, I watched Dawkins snap his toe down hard on the edge of the tray where it lay on the floor. It popped into the air and he caught it just as Mr Clean thrust his sword. The man's blade sank three inches into the tray, then stuck.

"Fibreglass!" Dawkins said, wrenching the tray sideways and yanking Mr Clean's sword from his opponent's hand. He dropped the impaled tray and casually walked forward, swishing the point of his spadroon left and right.

Mr Clean turned and ran to the bathroom, folding the accordion door shut behind him and locking it.

"Fine," Dawkins said. "You can just stay in there."

Floss Hair's pockets were mostly empty – his train ticket and a set of keys in his front pockets, and in his back pocket, a wallet and a photo of me from seventh grade.

"Why does this guy have this dopey picture of you?" Greta asked.

"I wish I knew," I answered.

"We should restrain him," Greta said. She slid out the man's belt, then pulled his arms behind him, looping the belt around his wrists and tying a complicated knot.

"Where'd you learn to do that?" I asked. It didn't fit with the Greta I knew. She was one of those girls who sat in the front row and always had her hand up before the teacher finished asking the question.

"My dad's in the FBI," she said. "As you'd know if you ever paid attention to anyone at school."

"My mom kept me busy," I protested, but it sounded like a lame excuse even to me.

Meanwhile, Dawkins had slid the sword through the bathroom door handle like a crossbar. The guy inside jiggled it; the sword rattled in place but didn't come loose.

Dawkins walked over to us, dusting off his hands. He eyeballed Floss Hair's belt-bound hands. "That your idea?" he asked Greta. When she nodded, he smiled and said, "Strong work."

At that moment, the floor rocked and tilted, and the air was filled with a long metallic wailing. "Oh, for crying out loud," Dawkins said. "They're stopping the train." He helped us to our feet. "Come on, we need to be ready to disembark once it's stopped. Before more of our friends board."

"Go ahead," Greta said. "I'm staying here."

"I'm sorry, darling, but you're coming with us."

She crossed her pale arms and raised her chin. "No, I'm not."

Looking at her flushed face and glittering green eyes, I believed she was stubborn enough to fight Dawkins. "Let's just leave her be," I told him.

But Dawkins shook his head. He bent and wrenched loose the sword that was stuck in the dining tray. "Listen, Greta. These two galoots who came in here? They're just two of an army." As if to confirm this, the bathroom door rattled. "The people who come *after* this lot are going to be much meaner."

"I can handle them," Greta said. "Tell him, Ronan."

"She *can* be pretty tough," I said, remembering how at the start of seventh grade she'd humiliated three massive kids who'd been trying to push around a smaller boy. (*Me*, that is. I'd protested that I didn't need her help, that I was a better fighter than I looked, but she just told me to shut my mouth and let her save me.)

"I'm sure she's tougher than steel-studded shoe leather, but that won't matter." He turned to Greta.

"They're going to believe you're partnered with me and Ronan here. And they're going to hurt you. A *lot*. I can't allow that, so, like it or not, you *are* coming with us."

Greta quietly surveyed the wreckage around us. "OK," she said.

"This is everything the guy had." I handed over the keys, ticket and wallet. And, feeling strange about it, my photograph.

"Thanks, Ronan," Dawkins said, "but I already know what you look like."

"*He* had it," I said. "Why does he have a picture of me?"

"A very good question," Dawkins said. Flipping through the key ring, he came across a black metal cylinder with a button. "Why, lookie here."

"What's that?" I asked.

"A luggage fob," Dawkins said. He pocketed everything else, then gestured for Greta to lead the way. "After you, Miss Sustermann. But don't try making a break for it or I'll run this sword through Ronan here." He grimaced and mimed skewering me.

Greta rolled her eyes, shoved open the door, and we followed her out.

"What's the big deal with the luggage whatsit?" I asked.

"It's like an electronic key for a car," Greta said. "The suitcase beeps when you press it. Helps you find your bag."

"Those two were likely put on the train in case you slipped the noose of that group at the station," Dawkins said. "This key fob means they brought toys."

While we'd been in the dining car, the terrain had changed. Gone were the leafy green suburbs. Instead, I saw low, flat plains covered with dark scrub. A busy highway ran parallel to the tracks, with all the usual junky buildings that pop up around highways – gas stations and fast-food joints and big grey car parks. Reminded me of a road trip I'd taken with my parents back when I was nine, before my dad's job changed, before his work had swallowed him up.

Thinking of my dad made me wonder about Greta's family and her interrupted phone call. "Where are your parents anyway?" I asked.

"They got divorced last year," she said. "Now my dad lives in DC. I'm going to visit him for a long weekend."

I heard myself saying, "That sucks," because sometimes that's all you can say.

"You know what sucks even more?" Greta asked.

"Being taken hostage by a kid from my old class and his smelly pickpocket friend."

"He's not my friend!" I insisted.

"I'm *right here*, you two," Dawkins said loudly. "I can *hear* you."

That was when I became hyperaware of the quiet: no one in the car was saying anything. The passengers were silent, cowering as far away as possible, parents clutching their children, everyone desperate not to be noticed by—

By us.

Then I realized why: not only was Dawkins covered with gobs of cheese and splats of ketchup and mustard, but he was still holding that big sword in his hand. A sword that flickered with a faint light all its own. And to top it off, he was smiling that loopy grin of his. We must have looked like a parade of lunatics.

A *bleep* trilled out from somewhere up ahead: a luggage rack with two expensive-looking black cases – a leather satchel about the size of a backpack and a larger duffel bag. "These will be ours," Dawkins said, heaving the duffel at me.

I caught it – just. It was heavy and clanked like it was full of scrap metal.

"You can't just take their luggage," Greta protested.

"Oh, yes, I can. They tried to stick us with those swords. The least they can do is give us whatever it is they brought with them." Grabbing the satchel, Dawkins gestured towards the back of the train. "Move along."

In the next car, we came face to face with the moustachioed conductor. The man raised his hands in surrender.

"I'm very sorry, sir," Dawkins said, the sword pointed directly at the conductor's heart, "but I'll be needing your keys." Without a word, the man unclipped a big key ring from his belt and handed it over. "Many thanks," Dawkins said. "Now we'll just get out of your hair."

I glimpsed my backpack in the overhead rack as we passed, but there was nothing in there I needed, only my school stuff, so I left it where it was.

We went through one more car full of people. Outside, the landscape was barely crawling by; another few minutes and the train would be at a complete stop.

At the car's end, Dawkins unlocked a windowless door and ushered us inside. The baggage car was packed floor to ceiling with cages full of boxes and trunks. A narrow aisle led straight between them to a windowed door at the back of the train.

Greta and I peered out through the dirty glass, watching the tracks unspool behind the train like two long strands of silver ribbon.

"The end of the line," Greta said. She rearranged some pins in her fire-red hair. "I've thought it over, and there is no way I'm getting off this train with you two." She stared at Dawkins. "Are you going to stab me to get through this door? I don't think so."

"That is not the door we'll be leaving by," said Dawkins. He wrenched a big lever back, and part of the wall slid out and aside like the door on a minivan. Now we were standing along the edge of a wide empty space, being buffeted by the wind. The train tracks sat high on a gravel-covered embankment. A dozen feet below us, the ground moved past in a colourful rush.

The noise was deafening – the sharp whine of the brakes, the banging of the train wheels, the air blasting into the car. Greta's ponytail blew apart, obscuring her face in a cloud of red.

"I reckon we're going no faster than ten miles an hour," Dawkins shouted. "The train will be at a full stop shortly." He tossed the satchel he'd been holding out the door. It tumbled end over end before disappearing in a thorny bush. Then he took the duffel bag from me and threw it after the first, along with the sword he'd been holding.

Resting a hand on my shoulder, Dawkins leaned close to my ear. "The trick to not getting hurt is to keep your arms and legs close to your body and just let yourself roll."

"Getting hurt?" I repeated. "Once we stop it won't—"

Dawkins' hand clenched my shoulder hard, and with his other hand he grabbed the waistband of my jeans. Before I knew what was happening, I was airborne.

He'd thrown me off the train.

CHAPTER SIX

ALL MESSED UP AND NO PLACE TO GO

A half second later, my feet slammed into the gravelly embankment and I fell forward, hard. What happened next might be called "rolling", but that sounds like I had some control over it.

I screamed the whole time.

After a few seconds, I came to a stop and lay there hacking, the wind knocked out of me. I'd skinned my hands and I had dust in my mouth and eyes, but I didn't think I'd busted anything.

As the screech of the train's brakes faded away, I heard something else: indignant yelling. Twenty feet away, Greta was sitting cross-legged in the dirt, pounding her fists against her knees and hollering curses until she ran out of air.

Then Dawkins himself leaped out. He tucked himself into a ball, did a perfect little roll like some kind of martial arts movie star, and came up on his feet. He clapped his hands against his clothes to shake off the dust, then jogged our way, waving happily.

As he came nearer, Dawkins called out, "Sorry about that, you two – but there wasn't time to ease you into it."

"You threw me from the train!" I shouted.

"Right. And this is me apologizing. Now let's go collect the luggage and clean ourselves up." He dusted off my shoulders. "You look OK to me. How are you feeling?"

"Bruised."

"You guys are in so much trouble," Greta muttered. She took her phone out of her pocket and began typing on it again – probably finishing the text to her dad.

With a yell, Dawkins plucked the phone from her hands, dashed it to the ground, and then stomped on it. There was a sad, soft, crunching sound.

Greta worked her jaw silently for a moment before finally blurting out, "You ruined my phone!"

"Yeah, sorry," Dawkins said. "There's GPS in those things, you know."

"What, you think they won't figure out you jumped off the train?" she said, raising her fists and swinging at him like she knew what she was doing.

"Easy there, slugger!" Dawkins said, skittering backwards and raising his palms. "Sure, they'll know we've scarpered, but I'd rather not make locating us *too* easy. So no phones." He pointed across the scrubby plain, to a sprawling truck stop alongside the highway. "Come on – I thought we'd go to that petrol station yonder." There were several low-slung buildings and petrol pumps, all of them crowded with articulated lorries and cars. The place was busy. Even from this distance I could see people milling about like ants on a countertop.

Beside me Greta said, "This guy is super corn nuts crazypants. You get that, right?"

"Whatever gave you that idea?" I asked.

"Don't get smart with me, *Evelyn* Ronan Truelove."

"He saved us when those guys attacked us with swords."

"What makes you think they were after *us*? Did it occur to you that maybe they were after *him*? He's a thief! He smells! He has the phoniest British accent I've ever heard. There are probably *thousands* of people who'd like to skewer him."

As I slogged along beside her, I couldn't decide whether to tell Greta about my mom, about the people in the train station. Back in New York, we'd never exactly been friends. "It's more complicated than that."

"No, it's not. It's simple," she said. "We go with him to the truck stop, and then when we see a chance, we get help. My dad will save us."

Watching the back of Dawkins' dirty brown leather jacket as he picked his way along the embankment, I thought maybe this was how he'd got so dirty. He probably jumped from trains all the time.

"Success!" Dawkins cried from ahead, raising the satchel in one hand and the duffel bag in the other. "I've got a good feeling about what's in these bags," he called out, "but why don't we wait until we've crossed the road to check them out."

"Sure thing," Greta said, giving Dawkins a look. "Whatever you say."

"As you pointed out, it won't take our foes long to deduce we've left the train," Dawkins said. The train sat on the tracks several hundred yards away. Several vehicles had pulled up alongside it – familiar red SUVs that seemed to almost glow in the late-afternoon sun.

"So maybe we should all . . . run!" he chirped, sprinting away.

Greta groaned, but we both took off after him.

When you're in a car, you don't notice how big car parks can be. You roll down one row after another until you find a spot close to the doors of wherever you're going, and then you complain because you have to walk for a whole minute. But imagine starting from the furthest edge of the biggest mall car park you know, one that stretches on like the scorched surface of some tar-covered planet.

Jogging across the endless truck stop with Dawkins and Greta, I felt naked, exposed, certain that the red SUVs would come skidding to a halt around us before we made it even halfway to the buildings.

But that didn't happen. Instead, we just got sweaty and tired.

"Super," Greta muttered. "And now I'm going to be sunburned too."

We reached the main building, a sprawling gas station/convenience store/food court/novelty emporium. At an angle to it was another building, a garage with half a dozen enormous raised doors and four more closed ones, the shadowy hulks of big lorries and cars dimly visible inside. In front of both buildings were triple rows of pumps, eight to a row, with lines of cars and trucks pulling in, filling up and zooming away.

Dawkins led us into an alley between the two buildings, where reeking skips were parked along the back walls. "I don't think anyone noticed us crossing over here," he said, peeking back around the corner and dropping the two bags.

"I don't know." Greta fanned herself with her hand. "You don't see that many people running across a car park. We probably stuck out."

"Sure," he said, crouching down over the bags. "But people have what psychologists call 'selective perception'. You see something that doesn't make sense and your brain works hard to make it fit in with everything else you're looking at."

"If you say so," Greta said, but she was edging back the way we'd come.

"Let's see what those two on the train were packing." The first things he Dawkins pulled out of the black leather satchel were – "Tighty-whities!" he announced. And vests and dark socks, all of which he flung over his shoulder, straight into the trash. They made soft *pongs* against the metal wall of the skip.

"What are we waiting for?" Greta whispered to me. "Let's move. *Now*."

"Interesting," Dawkins said, pulling forth a sort of plastic pistol-looking thing with a squat square black barrel, like a laser blaster in an old science-fiction movie.

"What's that?" I asked.

"Looks like a Taser," Greta said, biting her lip.

"It is *not* a Taser," Dawkins said. "I've heard about these but never actually seen one. It's a kind of electrical pulse weapon they call a Tesla gun."

"What does it do?" I asked.

"No idea." He set the Tesla gun on the ground, then fished out some shiny handcuffs and a huge black pistol. The last thing in the satchel was an old-school silver lighter. "A Zippo. Don't see these much any more." He snapped the lid open and rolled the striker. A flame appeared.

"Can we go inside now?" Greta said.

Dawkins made a face at her. "Not until we find their money." He snapped the lighter shut and pocketed it, then dragged over the duffel bag.

Swaddled within it were swords – six of them. "Yeesh, these guys were packing some serious fighting gear,"

Dawkins said, pulling them out. He heaved the swords into the skip, along with a phone he found – after first tearing out its battery. "So, Greta Sustermann," he said, "you probably think those fellows on the train were after me."

"I sure didn't invite them to the party," Greta said, stepping backwards.

"They were after Ronan," Dawkins explained. "Which is why they had his picture. That's because his mother is part of a secret society of . . . protectors, I guess you'd call them. Her enemies can't get to her, so they're pursuing her son."

Greta snorted. "Mrs Truelove works at a museum, not as a – whatever you called it – a secret protector. And if it's so secret, why are you telling me about it?"

"Sometimes secrets need to be told to keep people safe," Dawkins said, rooting around again in the duffel bag.

"Don't take this personally," Greta said, pivoting towards the head of the alley, "but you are completely out of your mind."

"He's telling the truth," I said quietly, remembering my mom knocking bullets aside with a sword and then leaping through the air. If I were Greta, I wouldn't have trusted Dawkins either. But I didn't doubt my mom for one second. "It's called the Blood Guard. My mom told me about it just before she disappeared."

"Ronan!" Dawkins snapped. "You know that calling something *secret* means you're not supposed to blab about it, right?"

"But you just did!" I protested.

"True enough," he said. "Getting sloppy in my old age."

"Does it matter?" I asked, bewildered.

"No, it doesn't," Greta said. "Trust me – I'm not going to tell anyone about these people who guard blood."

"The name isn't literal," Dawkins said, exasperated. "It's an age-old, clandestine honour guard of soldiers who dedicate their lives to protecting the hidden Righteous Ones."

Hearing it said like that, from someone other than my mom, made something catch in my throat. Maybe my mom had led a secret life, but it was secret for a reason. For honour. To protect someone else. *I'm one of the good guys, Ronan*, she'd said. *And so are you.*

"'Hidden Righteous Ones'?" Greta said, turning to me. "Do you hear how loony this guy sounds? He's paranoid and delusional."

"No, he's not," I insisted. "My mom *is* one of the Blood Guard. She told me. That's why those people took my dad – to try and get at my mom. And that's why they're after me now."

"Wait." The anger in Greta's face vanished. "Something happened to your dad?"

"Yeah," I said, and I didn't even care that my voice wavered. "My mom said he was taken – kidnapped – by those people on the train."

"I'm sorry about your dad, Ronan," Greta said. "I really am. And about whatever's going on with your mom."

"They're going to be OK," I said, more to myself than to Greta. I thought again of how my mom took out the fake cops. "She's a lot tougher than she looks."

Greta gave me a tight smile. "Good. But I'm leaving now. I'm going in there and calling the police." She turned.

"Please, Greta," Dawkins said. "Not yet. Just let us get away first. I give you my word I won't allow you to be hurt—"

"You threw me from a moving train!"

"OK, that was kind of bad, but it wasn't moving *that* fast." He put the duffel bag down, picked up the pistol and handed it to her butt-first. "Here, take this as an insurance policy. You know how to use one of these, don't you? Your dad must have trained you."

Without a moment's hesitation, Greta took the pistol. There was a rapid bunch of loud clicks, and within a few seconds the pistol was a pile of parts in her hand. She chucked most of the parts into the trash, but the top piece — the barrel — she threw with all her might into the field behind the buildings.

"What did you just do?" I asked in confusion.

"Disassembled it. Guns are bad news, Ronan." I must have looked amazed, because she said to me, "What? I told you — my dad's in the FBI. Since we have guns in the house, he insists I know how to use them. *Safely.*" She pointed at Dawkins. "You see, Ronan? Your friend gives *guns* to *kids.* What kind of responsible person would do that?"

"Lot of good that pistol's going to do anyone now," Dawkins said, but he was smiling a little, almost like he was pleased. And then he withdrew his hand from the duffel, holding a two-inch-thick roll of twenty-dollar bills. "Cha-ching!"

"'Cha-ching'?" Greta repeated to me, a pleading look in her eyes. "Really?"

Dawkins dropped the money and Tesla gun into the satchel, stood up and threw the empty duffel bag into the trash. He dragged a hand through his greasy hair and rubbed vigorously at his face. He looked exhausted. "Our enemies don't know who you are or that you're with us, Greta, so you should be safe once Ronan and I depart. But that will work only if you agree to hold off calling your father until we've made our escape. Deal?"

Greta looked back and forth between us, then finally growled with exasperation. "Deal. But I'm only doing this because I don't want to make it worse for Ronan's parents."

Dawkins broke into that crazy smile of his. "Then it's time to find ourselves a ride!"

CHAPTER SEVEN

THE RIGHT MAN FOR THE WRONG JOB

Dawkins instructed us to clean ourselves up while he attended to "more urgent tasks".

"Since when do you care about cleanliness?" Greta asked him, sniffing loudly.

"Yes, yes, very clever," he said. "If we're going to avoid suspicion in this place, you have to look well-scrubbed and not like you're running for your life."

The men's room was enormous, with dozens of stalls and showers. I cleaned myself up as best I could at one of the many sinks and tried not to catch anyone's eye, remembering what had happened the last time I was in a men's room.

When I came out, I found Greta at a table in the

dining area, her red hair dripping wet. She was busy pinning it back and pulling it through her scrunchie. It looked complicated.

"Why don't you just cut your hair short?" I asked.

"I like it long," she said, sliding a barrette into place as she stared at me. "So spill: who are those people with the swords?"

"I wish I knew," I replied, feeling frustrated. "I need to find out from Dawkins. But they're the same ones who've been chasing me since my mom put me on the train in Stanhope."

I gazed around the truck stop, wondering how long we had until the bad guys caught up with us. There were a lot of older men in rumpled jeans and baseball caps browsing the junk for sale, clearly truckers taking a break from the road. But there were also families, killing time while they filled up their cars. From overhead came the soft twang of country music. The entire place was busy and noisy, and nobody paid us any attention at all.

The hands of an old-style clock over the registers showed the time: just after six o'clock. "It's dinnertime," I said, wishing I was about to sit down with my parents.

"It's *time* to call my dad," Greta said. "Give me your phone."

"But you made a deal with Dawkins!" I said.

"I'm not going to break my word," Greta said. "I just want to let my dad know I'm all right."

I patted down my pockets and then remembered: my phone was in my backpack on the rack above my seat. I closed my eyes. "I'm so dumb; I left it on the train."

"Super," Greta said, pouting out her lower lip and blowing her wet hair away from her forehead. "I seriously don't trust this guy, Ronan. And you shouldn't either." The Greta I'd known back at school had always been pretty but with a hardness to her, like a fingernail slick with red polish. She didn't seem that way now. Her clear green eyes looked worried. For *me*. "There were a couple of pay phones back there by the bathrooms. I'm just going to call my dad and tell him I'll wait for him here. OK?"

This wasn't her fight or her problem. I was just some stupid kid from her old class who she tried to help once upon a time. "Sure," I said.

The smile that lit up her face made her look pretty – so much so that I had to look away. "Great!" She was out of the booth and had vanished before I could even think about trying to stop her.

*

Moments later, Dawkins slid in across from me. "We're good to go. Where's Sustermann?"

"Bathroom, I think," I lied.

"Still? *Girls.* Anyway, I found a guy who is happy to give us a lift as far as Roanoke, Virginia."

"Roanoke?" I said. "We're supposed to be going to DC!" Maybe Greta was right and my mom was wrong, and Dawkins *was* a madman. "Roanoke wasn't the plan."

"The plan has changed. Greta got mixed up with us, and then those two agents appeared, and – well, I've reconsidered the wisdom of our initial itinerary. They are too much up in our business, Ronan, and I don't know why." He drummed his fingers on the table. "I tried calling my contact on the pay phones back there, but wasn't able to get hold of him, which worries me a teensy-weensy bit."

"You're not listening," I said, feeling sick and out of control. I needed someone I trusted to tell me what to do. "My mom told me to go to DC, and Greta's dad lives there."

"And that's *exactly* why DC is such a bad idea, Ronan. Something very bad is going down, and for reasons I can't go into, it is best we get both you and Greta far away. So we're going to Roanoke."

"No," Greta's voice cut in, "we are not." She'd come up behind Dawkins while he talked. "Ronan, don't go with him."

I looked from her to Dawkins. Would my mom want me to go to Roanoke? I didn't even know where that was. Maybe my mom didn't know Dawkins. Maybe he wasn't a part of the Blood Guard at all. And yet he *had* known how to answer the question my mom told me to ask.

"Don't waste too much time making up your mind, Ronan," Greta said. She looked upset; I wondered what she'd told her dad. She held up the weird-looking Tesla gun from Dawkins' satchel. "Oh, and I'm taking this. Just to make sure no one gets hurt."

She tucked it into her waistband, pulled her shirt over it and marched outside.

Dawkins and I stood up at the same time.

"What are you going to do?" I asked him.

"Nothing." He held me back with a palm against my chest. "Her dad will sort her out soon enough. She's safer apart from us anyway. It's you they're after, Ronan, and so long as they don't know about Greta, she'll be OK— Oh, for the love of Pete."

He grabbed my arm and jerked me right, towards a

row of claw machines and pinball games and a photo booth with a little blue curtain.

But we didn't move so fast that I'd missed what he'd seen: as Greta opened the glass double doors at the front of the building, she was stopped by three people. Two men in natty dark blue suits and a severe-looking older blonde woman.

"The lady from the station. And the bald guy from the train," I said, hoping Dawkins hadn't heard me gulp. The other guy had long black hair that had been greased back against his scalp.

"Right." Dawkins shoved me inside the photo booth. Then he stepped in after me, yanking the curtain shut. "Well, there goes a good plan."

"What do you mean?"

"I mean, we're not going anywhere now." He peeked out. "We've got to go rescue our mouthy little friend."

"She's not my friend," I protested.

Dawkins gave me a look of such withering contempt that I immediately felt ashamed. "Of course she is. Do you know why those three haven't come back here yet to nab us? Because even though they've grabbed Greta, she hasn't told them where we are. She probably lied and that's why they're looking for us outside.

"So we've got to go rescue her," Dawkins added, crouching down and sliding through the curtain. "Come on. Stay low." He led me deeper into the truck stop. Beyond the restaurant area the store extended in every direction, like the biggest convenience store in the world. In the back corner was a dark doorway curtained with long clear strips of heavy plastic. "Storeroom," he said, pointing. "Should lead outside."

Four crates of milk were stacked on a trolley beside the plastic-strip curtain. Dawkins tipped the trolley back on its wheels and rolled it through the doorway.

A chubby young guy in a blue apron glanced at us as we passed, but the trolley must have convinced him we belonged, because he just turned back to stocking an ice-cream case.

Dawkins pushed the trolley through another strip curtain and into a giant room with ramps and a parked truck — a loading bay. There were slots for trucks to back into, and huge roll-up doors open to the outside. Dawkins left the milk on the nearest ramp and peered around one of the doors. I joined him.

"She's resisting," he said. "Scrappy little thing, that girl."

A red SUV was parked on a raised cement island

between the two filling stations, its doors hanging open. The blonde woman, her two minions, and Greta were struggling in front of it. Even from here, I could hear Greta shouting that her dad was a cop, that they were going to be in huge trouble, that if they were smart they'd get him on the phone before it was too late.

All of the people filling up their cars had stopped what they were doing, but the woman held up a silver badge in a leather wallet and began talking.

"What's she saying?" I asked.

"Probably identifying herself as police or some other nonsense," Dawkins muttered in disgust. "People are easily duped by official-looking shiny things."

The slicked-back hair guy put Greta in handcuffs, and then he and Mr Clean lifted her into the back seat and locked the cuffs around an armrest. She kicked and screamed the whole time.

"I wish she hadn't taken that Tesla gun," Dawkins said.

"Why?" I asked.

"Because now Blondie and her goons have it," he replied.

The woman Dawkins called Blondie handed Mr Clean the weapon, and he leaned back in the open door of the SUV. Then Blondie and Slicked-Back Hair separated. She headed right, towards the garage/ auto-shop area, and he came our way, disappearing among the line of lorries waiting to fill up at the diesel pumps.

"Now's our chance," Dawkins announced, sidling outside. Crouched low, he ran around the corner. I followed as quickly as I could, wondering why we were going in the opposite direction from Greta and hoping that the blonde lady – wherever she'd gone – wouldn't see us.

But I didn't hear any shouts or gunshots, and then it didn't matter any more, because we'd turned another corner and were deep in the shadows of the garage.

The place stank of old oil and gasoline, and there was junk all over the place – teetering stacks of tyres and grime-encrusted car parts heaped against the walls. An engine was suspended in a harness of chains, a black puddle of gunk beneath it. An enormous rusty orange Cadillac sat right in the entryway, the rear end propped up on a rickety pair of tyre jacks. It didn't have any back wheels, just rusty metal discs where the tyres should have been, lug nut screws sticking out. A panda bear key chain dangled from the ignition.

"Nice ride," Dawkins commented. "Keep an eye out, Ronan. We need something we can use as a weapon."

A friendly-looking old man in a spectacularly dirty grey jumpsuit walked up, wiping his hands on a greasy rag. "May I help you two young gentlemen?" he asked. Sewn on to his chest was a name patch that read ALBIE.

"Why, hello!" Dawkins said brightly. "We're here to pick up our 1985 Oldsmobile Cutlass Supreme. Brought it in to have the head gasket replaced."

I didn't even have to look to know that Dawkins had turned on that smile of his. Albie grinned in response. "I don't recall an Olds with a blown gasket, but let me go find the paperwork in the office. May take me a minute; it's a mess in there."

"Sure, go ahead," Dawkins said. "We're in no rush."

But we were – Blondie and her goons would be here any minute. I jiggled my leg and tried not to look anxious.

After Albie disappeared, Dawkins picked up a tyre iron and smacked it against his palm, then sighed. "It's no use. The problem is, they're right out there in the centre of the car park, so that guy will see us coming from a mile away."

"Right," I said. "My mom — she ran really fast. Can you maybe do the same thing? Magic?"

"Can I do *magic*?" Dawkins said, disbelieving. "You mean like flap my wings and *fly* out there? Or turn invisible?"

"That sounds kind of dumb, doesn't it?"

He replaced the tyre iron. "The Guard can't fly or turn invisible, Ronan. I suppose the speed thing *is* magic of a sort," Dawkins said, "but it's a talent that would be useless here. He'd still see me coming, and even if I dodged the shot from his weapon, he might harm Greta."

"Oh, right," I said. "Greta."

"We need to be sneaky but get to her fast."

"How about that thing over there?" I pointed to what looked like a short ambulance stretcher on wheels. It had a cushion for someone's head, and a four-foot-long platform — a creeper that mechanics lie down on to go underneath cars.

He put a foot on the creeper, rolling it back and forth. "Good idea," he said, clapping me on my shoulder. "This looks like it should work."

"You're going to skateboard out there?"

"No, no," Dawkins said, bending down and picking it up. "I'm going to scoot out there on my belly. He'll never see me coming." He walked to the front of the garage, hugging the creeper to his chest. "But just to be sure, we'll need a distraction so big that Blondie and her goons won't see me either."

We looked out at the SUV. Between it and us were a few hundred yards of concrete, empty save for the occasional car or truck rumbling past.

"Where are you going to find a distraction that big?" I asked, feeling a bit uneasy. I had an idea where this was going.

"It's going to have to be completely bonkers, Ronan — something loud and maybe a little dangerous and just a whole lot insane." Dawkins smiled at me and threw an arm around my shoulders. "Which is to say, you're the perfect man for the job."

CHAPTER EIGHT

WHEELS OF MISFORTUNE

I'd never driven a car before, but Dawkins assured me it was easy. "A car like this one," he said, pointing to the orange Cadillac, "practically drives itself!"

"It doesn't have any back wheels," I pointed out.

He waved his hands as though this were no big deal and yanked open the Cadillac's door. "It's a front-wheel drive."

I thought of Greta out there, handcuffed and alone. "OK," I said, sliding into the driver's seat and snapping on the seat belt.

"First, you're going to turn that key there. That starts the engine."

"I said I hadn't driven before. I didn't say I was stupid."

"Then you put your foot on the brake – that's the wide centre pedal – and you're going to move the gearstick – this knob here – from *P* to *D*. The *D* stands for *drive*. At that point, you're good to go."

The world through the dirty windscreen was streaky and faraway. "I can't really see."

"What's to see? It's a truck-stop car park." Nonetheless, Dawkins spat on the glass and rubbed it with the sleeve of his leather jacket – smearing the dirt but clearing some space on the glass.

"So then I accelerate?"

"You're going to need to accelerate a *lot*. Really stomp on the pedal. Just go for broke."

"Key, brake, *D*, accelerate. Got it." I played through it in my head.

"Just aim straight ahead, past that line of cars at the pumps and right on to the open road beyond. Trust me, before you even get close, I'll have reached the SUV, taken out that bald number and freed Greta. Then she and I will come fetch you."

I shook my head. "That's the stupidest—"

He tossed the black leather satchel on to the seat beside me. "Don't forget to bring that when you ditch the car. It's got our stuff." He cradled the mechanic's creeper in his arms. "Remember, *you're* the distraction. So honk the horn the entire time. Yell like a crazy person if you want. We want them looking at *you*, the idiot driving a car without tyres. Not at *me*, the guy skating in from the loading bay."

With that, he stooped over and dashed outside, back the way we'd come. From the angle the Cadillac was facing, I couldn't really see the SUV, but that was probably for the best. I pulled the door shut, locked it and turned the key in the ignition.

The car engine must have been big – really big. It made a world of noise.

I was so startled that it took me a few seconds to remember what I was doing.

As I shifted into drive, there was a pounding on the window. I screamed and let my foot up. The car rocked forward and the engine died.

Beside the driver's side window was Albie. "You get out of that vehicle *right now*, young man – do you hear me?" He jiggled the door handle.

I smiled, shrugged, and turned the ignition key again. This time I knew what to do. I kept my foot on the brake, shifted gears, then noticed Albie picking up the tyre iron Dawkins had discarded. He raised it up like he was going to swing it right through the windscreen.

I jammed my foot so hard against the accelerator my leg went numb.

The front tyres spun, throwing up a smoky cloud of burning rubber. For a moment, nothing happened. Then something seemed to catch, and the Cadillac leaped forward off the jacks.

I yelled in terrified surprise – and a little bit of excitement, to be honest. I was driving!

Until, that is, the car's back end crashed down on the concrete.

I hope I never find out what a car wreck sounds like, but I imagine it sounds a lot like the ear-splitting screech the Caddy made as it flopped into the car park.

Albie slammed his fist against the roof and cried out, "Stop! Please, stop! You're ruining a classic!"

But there was no going back. I punched the accelerator again.

The car barely moved.

I stood on the pedal with both feet to push it as hard as I could. The engine revved, whining louder and louder until finally the car began dragging itself forward.

It was like a thousand metal fingernails scraping down hundreds of chalkboards.

It moved in jerks and spasms, like a dying animal. The back rims caught on something, the front tyres spun and grey clouds of smoke obscured the windscreen, then suddenly the car surged forward, fat showers of sparks fanning up behind me. After twenty feet of this, Albie gave up and watched, peeking between his fingers.

Me, I kept my leg stiff against the accelerator, my shoulders braced against the backrest, and looked right.

There was no sign of Dawkins. Everyone else was motionless, staring at the Cadillac: truckers at the diesel pumps, parents with their kids, the pump attendants in their pale blue work shirts, and Greta and Mr Clean. The SUV was more than a hundred yards away, parked between the fuelling stations, but I could see their faces easily. Which meant, I guess, they could totally make out my face too.

Mr Clean recognized me and began walking my way, his arm outstretched, aiming the blunt end of the Tesla gun.

I didn't hear the first shot because the noise of the metal undercarriage scraping the concrete was so loud.

But I *saw* it.

A jagged beam of bright purple electricity stretched through the air from the gun, crackling past the front of the Caddy's grill like a sideways lightning bolt. It left a bright afterimage in my vision.

I blinked, then looked back in time to see Mr Clean aim again. Right at my face.

I ducked. The inside of the car filled with light and a smell like burnt wiring, and all the hair on my arms and head stood on end. A smoking hole as large as a grapefruit appeared in the passenger window.

Without lifting my foot from the accelerator, I slid all the way down in the seat. Now I couldn't see where I was going. The car kept up its lurch-and-stop progress across the car park, and I peeked up above the door just as Mr Clean, still walking my way, lifted the weapon for a third shot.

This time the bolt of electricity came sweeping across the hood, sawing through the space where my head would have been if I'd been sitting up. The windscreen shattered, showering me with little cubes of safety glass, and where the bolt hit metal, it threw off white-hot sparks.

I screamed, sure I was going to die.

The Caddy was too slow. There was no way I was

going to get away from Mr Clean and his blonde boss –
not without back wheels.

I risked another glimpse over the door and saw a dark
blur behind the gunman: Dawkins on the mechanic's
creeper, speeding across the car park to the SUV.

And then I had to duck again.

Tendrils of lightning crackled around the Cadillac's
passenger side. Thankfully, the massive door held
against whatever the Tesla gun threw at me.

The next time I looked, I saw Dawkins and Greta
pile out of the SUV. Dawkins grabbed the mechanic's
creeper, threw it to the ground, and then leaped atop it
like a skateboarder.

He rode it straight into Mr Clean's back, and they
both went down. Greta ran past them, toward the
Cadillac, waving her arms and shouting.

I turned off the ignition in time to hear her say,
"...Oh my god turn off the car before you set everything
on fire!"

I pulled the strap of the satchel over my head and
pushed open the door.

The Caddy had left a trail of deep gouges in the
concrete, and wide streaks of oil and petrol. They stretched
all the way to the garage, where Albie was still standing,

looking dumbstruck, the tyre iron dangling from his limp hand. I had driven less than a hundred feet.

"Sorry!" I shouted to him.

Greta ran up, panting. "Are you out of your mind? What kind of fool drives a car with no back tyres?"

There was a scorched hole through the door where the bolt of energy from the Tesla gun had struck. Another minute and it would have cut all the way through.

"Let's grab Dawkins and get out of here," I said.

But he and Mr Clean weren't done with each other.

Dawkins was sitting on Mr Clean's chest and throwing punches, but the guy took them in stride. He curled his legs up, hooked one around Dawkins' waist, and with a twist, wrenched him off.

"We've got to get that gun," Greta said, running towards something glimmering on the concrete.

She reached it just as Mr Clean and Dawkins rolled right up to where the truck stop entrance met the ramp from the highway.

I took a quick glance around for Blondie and Slicked-Back Hair, and that's when I saw what was headed our way.

"Hey!" I shouted at Greta as I ran towards her. But she wasn't listening.

Greta reached the Tesla gun, scooped it up and took a stance like a cop in a movie – feet wide, both hands around the weapon, arms locked. "Stop *now* or I'll shoot!"

"Greta!" I grabbed her collar in my fist and yanked her towards me, hard.

A wall of wind slammed us backwards against the concrete as a blue articulated lorry skidded past, its brakes locked. In its wake was a cloud of smoke thrown up by the skid.

We sat on the concrete, coughing.

"What happened?" Greta asked. She tucked the Tesla gun into her jeans, pulled her shirt down and staggered to her feet. Then she helped me up.

"Dawkins!" I called out. "Jack!" I waved the smoke away, but there was nothing to see: just an enormous lorry truck in the middle of the gas station entrance.

The driver had stopped his vehicle, but only after it had skidded over the spot where Dawkins and Mr Clean had been fighting. Had they escaped? Rolled to the other side, maybe? I jogged alongside the wheels, shouting, "Jack? Jack?"

Greta followed. "They got away, right? Ronan, tell me they weren't there when—" And then she shrieked and clutched my arm.

I saw what she was looking at.

An arm was sticking out from beneath a set of four giant tyres, the leather jacket unmistakable, the fingers of the hand relaxed and open. The wheels rested nearly flat on the concrete. Anyone underneath them wouldn't be getting up ever again.

We'd found Dawkins.

CHAPTER NINE

GRAND THEFT AUTO

I don't know how long we stood there, staring. Long enough that the lorry driver, a portly man with mutton-chop whiskers, swung down out of his cab and came to stand beside us. "They were in the *road!*" he kept saying.

"We have to get out of here," Greta said, dragging me backwards by the hood of my sweatshirt. "He's gone, Ronan. We can't help him."

"But. . ." I couldn't stop staring at Dawkins' empty hand. I felt sickened knowing that he was under those wheels, sure, but that was only part of it. Mostly, what I felt was alone. The only connection I had to my parents had been this crazy kid with the weird accent, and now he was gone.

"I'm going to be sick," I said.

"No, Ronan, you're not," Greta said, yanking my arm again. "You are going to come with me."

She pulled me past a bunch of senior citizens in bum bags and sun visors who were piling out of a turquoise tour bus and joining a thick ring of onlookers. In the commotion, everyone seemed to have forgotten about the Cadillac.

"Keep edging back," Greta said quietly beside me. "We'll disappear in the crowd."

"There they are!" someone said. "Take them, Mr Four."

A hand caught my right arm and twisted it back so hard that I yelped. I found myself face to face with Slicked-Back Hair.

Mr Four, I guessed.

He was clean-shaven, but weirdly kind of slack-jawed and waxy looking. I couldn't tell how old he was. Definitely past thirty.

He stared at me, unblinking, his eyes full of nothing – not hatred, not satisfaction at having caught me, just emptiness. I felt cold metal as he snapped handcuffs on to my wrists.

Next to him was Blondie. Her slow smile made my

mouth go dry. "Children, we're going to have to take you in for questioning." She held up her badge again, and the people around us cleared a space. "There's nothing to see here," she announced. "Just two officers of the law apprehending a couple of young criminals."

"Let *go* of me," Greta snapped, twisting and trying to break the woman's grip.

The woman smacked the back of Greta's head with her open palm, then plucked the Tesla gun out from under her shirt, saying, "Aha!"

Around us, the crowd murmured.

Spinning Greta around, Blondie cuffed her, too, and pushed her towards the SUV. Mr. Four followed suit, planting his hand between my shoulder blades and shoving so hard that I thought I was going to fall flat on my face.

Then I heard something strange: applause. The crowd of people around us was *clapping*. Just a few at first, but then everyone joined in. And why? Because they believed what the blonde woman had told them: that we were criminals. For some reason, I felt ashamed. I dropped my head as we crossed the car park.

But Greta wasn't so easily embarrassed. "Are you people kidding me? We're being kidnapped, you idiots – *ow!*" The woman smacked Greta again, and she fell to her knees on the hot concrete. Without another word, Greta used her cuffed hands to shove herself back up. She kept her head held high.

Greta was right: we weren't criminals. The people around us had no idea what was going on. "We've done nothing wrong!" I said – and got a sharp jab at the back of my head from Mr Four.

And then we'd reached the SUV. Mr Four and the woman pushed Greta in first, then me after her. They opened our cuffs and locked them around the armrests in the back seat.

"While we see to a few things," the woman told us, "you will be silent and will draw no attention to yourselves. Or there will be consequences."

Mr Four went to the rear of the SUV and dug out a couple of long black zippered plastic bags, like the sort people carry suits in. He followed the woman back across the broad car park to the truck.

After a minute, the lorry slowly moved backwards. Several minutes after that, Mr Four returned, hunched over beneath the weight of those two long black bags, one slung over each shoulder. They looked . . . full. Of something.

With a grunt, he heaved the bags into the back of the SUV. Then he closed the door. We were next. He rattled the chains on our cuffs to see if we were still locked up tight.

Then, without a word, he turned and headed back to the crowd.

"Was that what I think it was?" I asked, picturing the bags in the back and feeling queasy.

"I don't even want to know," Greta said. Suddenly her cuff was swinging loose on her arm. "But why don't we get away from here before they come back and show us."

"Wha— Hey, how'd you do that?" I asked, but then answered myself, "Oh, let me guess; your dad's—"

"Right. He taught me how to pick locks. These are standard-issue Peerless cuffs, an old-school brand that's a total cakewalk if you know what you're doing. Which I do." Clenched in her fingers was a crooked bit of wire that looked like one of the pins that kept her mess of red hair in place.

"Unlock me too!"

"No time." She climbed forward between the front seats and slid behind the wheel like she did this sort of thing every day. "We have to get out of here.

Those dumb jerks are so sure of themselves that they left the keys." She snapped the seat belt, adjusted the mirror and gently cranked the ignition. "Pull that door shut."

I slid the passenger door closed with my free hand as the engine came to life with a quiet rumble. In a moment, Greta had the SUV moving.

"Your dad taught you how to drive too?" I asked in disbelief, but she didn't answer. She nudged the accelerator and soon the SUV was rolling away like we had just stopped to fill up and were now getting back on the road.

I didn't realize I was holding my breath until I gasped for air.

"You all right back there?" Greta asked, her eyes on the road.

"I can't believe this," I said. "Are we really getting away?"

"I hope so," Greta said, glancing into the rear-view mirror and biting her lip. "Unless they have— Wow."

I twisted and looked over my shoulder. Through the smoky back window of the SUV, I could see the truck stop dwindling, everything getting smaller behind us. And I could see something else: the blonde woman and Mr Four running after us, keeping pace with the SUV.

"They're chasing us!" I shouted. "You have to go faster!"

When we reached the slip road, the blonde woman stopped. She stared after us, her hands on her hips.

Mr Four didn't slow down at all.

He ran with long loping strides. There were cars leaving the truck stop that he passed in a blur, dodging them like they weren't moving. When he came upon two cars driving side by side, he just hurdled them, sailing through the air and landing in stride. He kept coming.

"How can he move like that?" Greta asked. "What are these people?"

"I don't know," I said. "How fast can you push this thing?"

"I just hit thirty miles an hour," she said. "That's the speed limit for the slip road."

"Forget the speed limit," I said. "We need to lose this guy!"

He was moving faster than the traffic, bouncing from foot to foot, never slowing.

Greta punched the accelerator.

The SUV seemed to gather itself for a split second

before surging forward. Through the rear window, I could see Mr Four get smaller and smaller, until he was just a dot at the edge of the slip road.

We drove in silence for a minute.

"Who *are* those people?" Greta asked. "And why are they so hot to get you?" Her eyes caught mine in the rear-view mirror. "I mean, nothing personal, Ronan, but you're kind of an idiot."

"Thanks for that," I said, smirking. "Dawkins never got a chance to explain them to me. And neither did my mom." I knuckled my eyes with my free hand and hoped that the people who took my dad weren't anything like this woman and her crew. "I don't know anything more than you do."

"It's OK," she said. "My dad will help us. Once we find a phone."

"Didn't you already call him?" I asked. "Back at the truck stop?"

"He didn't answer. I left a message, but. . ." She drummed her fingers on the steering wheel. "Let's just concentrate on getting as far away from those people as possible. In a couple of hours we'll be at my dad's place and this nightmare will be over." She smiled anxiously at me in the mirror.

I watched as a pair of ambulances roared past in the opposite lane, their sirens blaring.

They were too late, I knew. I thought of poor Dawkins squished under a lorry like a bug under a boot and shuddered.

"We got away, Ronan," Greta said, her voice full of forced brightness. "We're safe now."

"Sure." I said, clanking my handcuffs. "We're safe."

I didn't believe it for a minute.

CHAPTER TEN

UP THE CREEK

An hour and a half later, with the sun sitting on the horizon, Greta steered us into the car park of an empty rest area.

"Why are we stopping?" I had no idea where we were. Somewhere near the border of Delaware and Maryland maybe, but I hadn't been paying close attention to the signs. "They could be right behind us."

"If I don't pee soon, I'm going to explode." She looked embarrassed as she turned off the engine. "Also? We're basically out of gas. They were so busy kidnapping us that they forgot to fill up the tank."

"Great," I said, looking out. The rest was nothing much – a little brick bathroom on a big slab of concrete, surrounded by a grassy area, some picnic tables and a dozen big streetlights that would probably kick on once the sunlight was gone. The grass sloped down to a narrow, reed-choked river, and a long way downstream a bridge spanned the water. It was almost peaceful.

I was as depressed as I had ever felt in my life. Here I was, out of petrol at an abandoned highway rest stop with a girl I barely knew, handcuffed to the back seat of a car stolen from the people who'd kidnapped my dad, chased my mom and killed the one person in the world who could explain to me what was going on. How long would it be until they caught up with me and Greta and killed us too?

"There's a pay phone on the wall over there. We'll use it to call for help. But first," Greta said, holding up the bent pin she'd used on her cuffs, "let's give you your freedom."

I checked out the pay phone while Greta used the toilets, but it wasn't going to be any help to us; there was no receiver on the end of the cord.

So we searched the SUV's glove compartment to see if there might be a mobile there, but it held only a couple of parking tickets and a manual for the car. Greta flipped through it, looked closely at the inside front cover and coughed. She showed me a bright red sticker reading THIS VEHICLE IS EQUIPPED WITH LoJACK.

"So what? What's that mean?"

"It's a tracking device for stolen cars. Basically it sends out a GPS beacon so that the car can be found by the police."

Suddenly I was all too aware of how alone we were. "That means they can—"

"Find us, yeah. They've probably already activated it."

"But that would take a while, right?"

"It would take a phone call. And a smartphone." She swallowed and looked around us at the deserted rest stop. "They're probably not that far behind."

"What should we do? Run? Go on foot?" We were trapped. There was no place to walk, just a thin line of trees along the highway. "Hitchhike?"

"Calm down, Ronan," Greta said.

"I'm calm!" I yelped, then realized she was right. I was panicking. I took a few deep, slow breaths. "OK, sorry. I am totally calming down now."

"Hitchhiking is way too risky. They'd probably be the ones to pull up and offer us a ride. We need to find a way to escape them so that they can't follow, and we need to call my dad and tell him exactly what is going on." Greta dropped the manual on the front seat. "Let's see what they've got in the back."

The storage compartment was packed. On the left was a long green trunk banded in steel, and snug against it were the two zippered black bags. Both were about as long as a person and lumpy. "Body bags," Greta whispered, stepping back. "They really are body bags. I didn't want to believe it." She leaned over, her hands on her knees, and breathed loudly. "Oh, man, I think I'm going to puke."

"I don't get it. Why would they pick up the bodies?"

"There's nothing to get, Ronan. These people are sick. Sick, sick, sick."

I didn't want to think about that. "At least now we have some money," I said. Sitting on top of the green trunk was the satchel Dawkins had given me. Inside was the Tesla gun (the woman must have put it there after she took it from Greta), the wad of cash and the Zippo lighter.

"What's this?" Greta pulled out something I'd forgotten: Dawkins' cheap spiral-bound notebook.

We flipped through the tattered pages. His scribbles

were tough to decipher. Some pages we just gave up on entirely. Towards the back, there was a note describing me – "black hair, short for his age, dark blue hoodie, yellow backpack, looks like Bree" – that made a lump form in my throat. *Bree* is my mom's name. And on the facing page: "3:41 southbound out of Stanhope."

"There's the proof that he did come because of my mom," I said, tapping the page.

"So he was telling the truth," Greta said. "Sorry I didn't believe you."

"It's OK. I wouldn't have believed us either."

There were sketches of various things and people, and lots of drawings of dogs. All kinds of dogs. We couldn't quite figure out one creepy illustration of a metal mask with three eyes, but the sketches of the blonde woman and two thugs in her gang were instantly recognizable. On the last page Dawkins had written the words MOUNT RUSHMORE all in caps.

He'd drawn a picture of the four sculpted president heads on the mountain, along with a fifth – his own grinning face, his long hair looking greasy even when carved in stone. Etched into the mountain below the heads were the words *Nunquam mori* – whatever that meant.

The rest of the pages were blank.

"What's it all mean?" I asked.

Greta threw the notebook and everything else back into the satchel. "That he's a bad artist? That he likes dogs? That he was completely nutso? Who knows."

She tried each of the keys on the green-metal trunk. The fourth slid in effortlessly and the lid opened on well-oiled hinges. She peeled away a big piece of foam packing material and for a few seconds, we just stared.

"Ronan," Greta finally whispered, "what exactly are your parents mixed up in?"

Inside the trunk were guns – nothing like any I'd ever seen before. I counted eight big black rifles and, tucked between them, pistols in holsters and other dark metal things that looked like weapons of one sort or another.

"They're not mixed up in anything," I said. "I mean, Dad's basically a big-deal accountant, and my mom—"

"These are modified SG 550s," Greta said, lightly touching the thick stock of one of the rifles, "and these look sort of like M14s, but these modifications" – she tapped the bulbous plastic swellings above the trigger guards – "I don't even know what those are."

"They look like that Tesla gun." I pulled it out of

Dawkins' satchel, and we compared them. I thought about those sideways lightning bolts shearing through the Cadillac's windscreen and shuddered. "Did you see what this thing did?"

"Yeah. Scary." She slammed the lid down and stepped away from the truck. "That is really evil stuff, Ronan. Guns? Body bags? We need to get rid of this stuff."

"We don't have time," I protested. "Why can't we just leave it in the truck?"

"Because when they catch up to us, they'll get all that evil junk back." She took my hands in hers. I don't know what I was expecting – girlishly soft fingers maybe – but her grasp was firm. "No one should have weapons like those things, Ronan. They're *horrible.*"

I turned to look out at the deserted rest stop. It felt like we were the only two people alive, like a horde of zombies might come running out of the bathrooms at any moment.

But here we were, stuck in the middle of nowhere, without any gas or a phone or anyone to help us. And a case full of scary-looking weapons. *What would my mom tell me to do?* I wondered. *What would Dawkins do?* The answer to that was easy: he'd help Greta.

"OK," I said. "Let's hurry. Grab the handle on the front end and I'll get the back."

The case was heavy, but it turned out to have wheels in the corners like a suitcase. We were able to roll it down the grassy slope to the bank of the river.

Greta slipped off her shoes and waded backwards into the water up to her knees.

"Can't we just throw it in?" I asked, but from the look on her face – her brows knotted together, her jaw gritted – I knew I'd have to wade in too. "OK, OK!"

On the first step, my foot sank in past my ankle. "Gross. There goes a good pair of sneakers."

"Should have taken them off before you got into the water, you big dope."

The case bobbed in the river, not floating exactly, but it didn't sink totally either. We just kind of steered it in the current.

At the halfway point, where the water was up to our armpits, Greta said, "This is good. Let go!"

The case drifted for a second before taking on water and vanishing. A fat air bubble rose up and was gone.

Greta said, "Just a sec." Then she took a deep breath and dived under.

I stood and waited. The sun sat on the horizon

and it made the water glint and twist around me like molten gold. A way upstream was a huge grassy meadow shifting in the wind, and further away, a tiny, weather-beaten grey cottage. Nearer to the river was a ramshackle white gazebo, with what looked like an old overturned canoe beside it.

Greta popped up with a gasp, then squeegeed her hair with her hands. "I opened the lid – wanted to make sure it stays sunk. And, you know, if those guns get ruined, all the better."

"That looks like a house over there." I pointed to the tiny cottage. "Maybe whoever lives there can help."

She stood in the water beside me, shading her eyes, and said, "That place looks like it hasn't been lived in since the Great Depression."

I squinted. Now I could make out the gaping black holes of the windows. "OK, so that wasn't the best idea."

"Why don't we take that canoe? Those people from the truck stop won't know where we went." Greta was dripping wet and shivering, her hair a soggy knot behind her head. She looked like a little kid, skinny and vulnerable.

"You're right," I said. "The canoe. Good idea."

"Duh, of course I'm right." She punched me in the arm and that whole vulnerable thing evaporated. "I'm *smart*, Ronan. One of us has to be."

Aluminium canoes, despite being made of the same stuff as drinks cans, are pretty heavy. It's a wonder they even float. We gave up trying to carry the canoe and instead just flipped it over, threw the satchel and the only paddle inside and dragged it to the water's edge. Greta got in front while I held it against the bank, and then I let go, hopped in the back, and just like that we were floating.

The current caught the nose of the canoe and turned us downstream. I picked up the aluminium paddle and slowly steered us towards the middle of the river.

"Check it out," Greta said, pulling a dented old hubcap from where it had been wedged in the frame. "I wonder why this is here?" It was as big as a salad bowl but shallow, a hubcap for a very old car – probably the same vintage as the abandoned house.

A trickle of water was filling the space in the bottom of the boat. "Probably for scooping out water – is this thing even seaworthy?"

Greta dipped the hubcap to the floor and raised it back up, full of water. "You paddle and I'll bail."

The noise of an engine caught our attention. It wasn't quite dark yet, but the car that turned into the rest stop had its headlights on. We were still a hundred yards upstream.

"Shhh," Greta said. "Let's just be quiet and drift past. Maybe they won't see us."

"You'd have to be blind not to see us," I said.

"Shhh," she repeated, tucking the hubcap under her arm and sliding down. "Maybe we can just lie inside and they'll think no one's in it?"

I hunched down too – into the water that was slowly flooding the canoe. "I'm getting *wet*," I said.

"You're already wet. Be quiet!"

We peeked over the canoe's edge as we drifted.

The car was a dark sedan with smoked-glass windows, like a million other cars. It circled the forecourt twice, finally pulling up beside the SUV. Doors opened; closed. I recognized the stiff gait of Mr Four, and the woman with her helmet of blonde hair. They came around the SUV, touched the hood – still warm, I bet – and then walked towards the rest stop bathroom.

We were almost past when the hubcap slipped out of Greta's grasp. It floated towards me in the shallow water in the canoe's base, bouncing off the sides and making little metallic clonking noises the whole way, until it came to rest against my feet.

I looked up from the hubcap into Greta's eyes. Her face had gone white.

"Evelyn Truelove!" the woman's voice called from the shoreline. "Is that you and your friend in that canoe?" She didn't sound angry at all; instead, her voice was concerned, like someone's worried mom.

I didn't want to answer, but it wasn't like she couldn't see us. And I needed to buy us time to drift further away. "Don't call me Evelyn!" I shouted, sitting up.

We were past the rest stop bathroom now, but not moving all that fast.

"Come back to shore," the woman said, ignoring me. Mr Four walked stiff-legged to the riverbank and fell to his knees in the shallows. He buried his hands and face in the water – drinking it? Washing?

I heard a loud *click* across the water.

"Gun," Greta whispered. "She just cocked the hammer of a pistol."

"I don't know what to call *you*," I yelled to the woman. "That doesn't seem fair."

"You can call me Ms Hand," the woman said. "Now come back to shore and we won't hurt you."

"I've got a better idea," I answered. "Why don't you come to us – the water's nice! Just ask Mr Four."

"Last warning, Evelyn."

"I told you, I don't like to be called—"

A bright flare of gunfire stopped me from finishing my sentence.

I couldn't see the bullet, of course, but I saw the muzzle flash, the upward snap of her wrist. She had aimed at Greta.

Something in my head took over and the paddle twirled in my hand.

There was a *clang*, the deafening sound of a ricochet and a numbing impact that I felt all the way up my arms.

Somehow I'd pivoted the paddle and deflected the bullet. Like I'd seen my mom do at the park earlier today.

From beside me, Greta whispered, "When did you learn to do *that*?"

I stared at the paddle with its puckered crater. "Never," I whispered. "I never learned to do that." I worked my fingers to make the numbness go away.

Ms Hand pointed to Mr Four and said, "Mr Four, use the sacrifice you've been given. I command you! Bend the water to your will!"

We couldn't see what Mr Four was doing, but we

could hear him: he was singing – chanting almost – at the river's edge. His voice was low and unsettling.

"Ronan," Greta said, her voice shaky, "something's happening."

"But we're almost away." It was true – we were past the entire rest stop now; there was no way they could catch us.

As Mr Four knelt and sang, his hands in the river, the water began to churn and splash and steam, as if he were holding something red-hot under the surface. Within moments, heaving waves began rolling underneath us, shouldering past our canoe as the water level dropped.

The water level was dropping upriver, too – boiling back away from where Mr Four was now on his knees in the mud, his arms held wide apart, his hands burning with red light. He almost seemed to be willing the water upstream and downstream away from the riverbed, clearing a widening strip of muddy river bottom that stretched all the way from one bank to the other.

The waters parted further and further until, with a wet slurp, our canoe came to rest in the mud. A few yards away, a fish gasped and flopped. Thirty feet downstream, a wall of water seethed against an invisible barrier. Upstream from Mr Four and Ms Hand was another wall of frothing water, this one twelve feet high and rising, dammed up by whatever magic Mr Four was working.

Kicking off her high-heeled shoes, Ms Hand walked out into the mud. She carried what looked like a long sliver of moonlight – a wide silver sword. Strange runes flickered on the blade, like those on the swords wielded against Dawkins by the guys on the train.

"I told you to come back," she growled between clenched teeth. "This has gone on long enough."

Behind her, Mr Four stayed as he was, kneeling, singing, continuing his whole Moses-parting-the-Red-Sea trick.

I looked at my paddle. I didn't like my odds against that sword. Meanwhile, Greta started to climb out of the canoe.

"Get back in," I said, standing up, feeling the canoe teeter beneath me. "It's Mr Four who's making this happen. We have to stop him." My foot came down on the hubcap.

I picked it up and thought of Dawkins with the tray in the dining car. *A Blood Guard finds weapons in whatever he has at hand.* I held the metal disc and felt the echo of a long-ago summer Frisbee league seize my brain.

I clenched my fingers along the metal rim of the disc in what Ultimate players call a power grip, cocked my wrist back and pivoted my arm behind me.

"Hold tight," I warned Greta.

She got down and wedged her hands and feet against the aluminium ribs of the canoe.

The moment she was secure, I snapped my wrist forward.

The hubcap flew straight and true, a long glimmering streak. Ms Hand swung as it passed, but missed, and then the hubcap connected with Mr Four's head. There was a sound like a big bell dropping to the ground, and he crumpled face forward into the mud.

With a roar Ms Hand charged towards us, lifting the sword over her shoulder for a mighty chop, trying to reach us before—

The river came back.

It hit with a huge *whomp*, water rushing in all around us.

Ms Hand was swallowed up completely.

At the same moment, the river flung our canoe into the air. The water flipped the back end straight up, right against me. Wedged tightly into the prow, Greta watched, her mouth wide in a soundless scream, as another wall of water smashed into us, straightening the canoe and slamming it back down so hard that it bounced.

I bounced with it, banging into the benches and struts, desperately clinging to the sides so that I wouldn't fall out.

Greta struggled to her knees while the canoe bucked and tossed and then, a minute later, it was over. The river was back to normal, rolling along serenely like nothing had happened.

We huddled in the bottom of the canoe, staring at each other in disbelief, both of us soaking wet and panting. Greta swiped her dripping hair out of her eyes.

I raised my head and peeked over the canoe's aluminium edge. The dammed-up water had rocketed us far downstream and now the rest stop was just a dark spot on the horizon. There wasn't a single sign of Ms Hand or Mr Four. Had they drowned? I stared for a while towards the place where they'd gone under, but I didn't see anyone surface.

We'd lost the paddle. For a moment I worried we'd lost the satchel too, but then I saw the strap over Greta's shoulder.

"Ronan?" Greta said. "Ronan, are you OK?"

"I think so?" I said. I watched until the rest stop had disappeared completely.

"What that guy was doing," Greta began, "that was . . . *magic*, wasn't it? And the way you blocked that bullet with the paddle? And threw that hubcap? This isn't just a load of scary people with guns, right? This is something else."

I remembered my mom, her legs a blur as she ran faster and leaped further than any human should be able to do. The men who'd been pursuing us – first at the train station and then at the truck stop – had done the same trick. And Mr Four, the partner – or the servant? – of Ms Hand, had parted the river, holding back a wall of water with just a song.

I turned to Greta and shivered in the darkness. "You're right. This is definitely something else."

CHAPTER ELEVEN

WE GET TAKEN FOR A RIDE

We'd been drifting quietly for a half hour or so — long enough for the shadows to swallow up the road and the river and us with it. Back in the city, streetlamps and car headlights and all the buildings can make you forget about how dark the night can get, but out here, the darkness was so heavy that I could barely see Greta sitting in the prow of the canoe, her body a shadow against the stars that were coming out across the sky.

I heard what sounded like a sob.

"Are you crying?" I asked.

"No," she said. "Just shut your stupid mouth, Ronan Truelove." But her voice had that giveaway full-of-snot-and-phlegm sound. "I've got allergies."

"OK."

"I mean, we got away, right? So what's to cry over?"

"Nothing I can think of," I said.

The river ran beside the road for a while, but then it turned east across the fields. I couldn't even see the traffic any more, could only hear a faint roaring noise that I figured was the highway.

Greta sniffed. "It's just . . . my parents split up and my mom is depressed, and I don't even get to see my dad unless I take the train to DC. It's like I don't even have a home any more." Greta gestured as she talked, rocking the canoe, and the water in the bottom sloshed around our feet. Now that the hubcap was gone, the boat was filling up, slowly but surely. "No offence, but I really wish I wasn't stuck in this canoe with you."

"No offence," I replied, "but I wish I wasn't stuck with you either." I wondered how my own parents were doing. Had Mom managed to escape Ms Hand's pals near the train station? "Actually, I'm sorry I got you mixed up in this."

"It's my own fault. If I hadn't been so high and mighty on the train, I wouldn't be involved."

"No," I said, "Dawkins had swiped that man's wallet, and you were just trying to do the right thing."

I heard a rustling and then a scratching noise, and suddenly I could see Greta clearly: she'd struck a flame with the Zippo lighter. It cast a warm glow over her face. "Dawkins' satchel is waterproof," she said.

"Great," I said and pictured Dawkins under the truck's tyres. I wished he were still with us. "What good is a lighter?"

"We could build a fire, maybe."

"In a canoe? On a river?"

"Once we get out of the canoe, dummy."

And then maybe the flame of the Zippo reminded her of something, because she asked, "So what happened to your family back in Brooklyn, anyway?"

"Our house burned down," I said. "I'm pretty sure you know that."

"Yeah, sorry about the arsonist comment earlier. I don't really think you set your own house on fire."

"Thanks for the vote of confidence."

"Though you have to admit it was pretty freakish how the place caught fire with you at home." She let the flame go out. "Do you think the fire had anything to do with why those people are after you?"

I stared at her in surprise. Was she right? Had the fire been because of the Blood Guard? Had my mom moved us to keep the family safe? Was the person my mother had been assigned to watch over – one of the thirty-six Pure Dawkins had talked about – one of our neighbours in Brooklyn?

"I'll ask my mom. If I ever see her again." I reached down and splashed my fingers in the dirty water in the bottom of the canoe. "We've taken on a lot of water. We should probably get to shore before we sink."

"Good idea." Greta craned her head around, looking at the dark banks rolling past. "Let's beach the canoe on the left up there," she said, "where it – wait! Ronan, look."

A shallow wall stretched across the entire width of the river up ahead. "What is it?"

"A dam," Greta said. She pointed to a patch of shoreline that was a smidge lighter than the surrounding night. "And I think that's a boat ramp over there."

"How do we get there?" I asked. It looked impossibly far away.

"We swim for it," she said. "It's not like we can get any wetter." She zipped up the pouches on Dawkins' bag. "On three?"

She counted out loud and together we flipped

ourselves into the freezing river. We swam to shore and climbed out on to a concrete apron that dipped down into the shallows.

The concrete was still warm from the afternoon sun. We stretched out on it and lay there panting, letting our bodies soak up the heat.

"So if Mr Four and Ms Hand got out of the river OK. . ." I said.

"Then they'll be really peeved."

We both laughed. But I was forcing it a little, worried again about how they'd parted the waters like that. Did any of us have a chance against people who could bend nature to their will?

"Seriously, though," Greta said. "If they did, they'd follow the river and check out every place we might stop."

"But the river stopped following the highway, like, an hour ago," I said, and got up. "They'd have to off-road it."

The dam wasn't much as dams go, just a long, thick concrete wall about twelve feet high that curved gently from one shore to the other. On the other side of it was a large reservoir that shone silver in the moonlight, and on its far edge, an empty car park. We had to climb a rusty chain-link fence to get to the top, and when we did, there wasn't a sign of life anywhere.

"Why's a lake need a car park?" I asked, pointing.

Greta looked at me like I was stupid and said, "Don't you ever go camping?"

"In a car park? No. In a tent in the woods? Totally."

"If you're in an motor home, you don't camp in the woods. You go to places like this. See? There are electric hook-ups and a shower block over there."

"That's not camping," I said. "That's . . . *parking*."

Two bright beams cut through the darkness.

"Car," Greta whispered.

There was a big green-metal utility box at the edge of the dam, and we crouched behind it, watching as the headlights roamed around the car park before pulling to a halt right in the centre.

I peeked over the utility box. It wasn't the red SUV or the car from the rest stop. It was just a long tan motor home, towing a small trailer that held a couple of motorcycles. As soon as it was parked, its running lights and headlamps went off, and the curtained windows along its length brightened with a warm yellow glow. "It's just a stupid motor home," I said.

Greta stood up. "Come on. Maybe whoever's in it has a phone."

We were thirty feet away when the side door of the motor home banged open. We flattened ourselves in the shadows and watched as a set of metal stairs extended from the side of the vehicle, and an overweight, grey-haired man in neon-bright shorts and flip-flops staggered out, two folded lawn chairs in his arms. "Won't take but a minute to set up," he called to someone inside.

He set the chairs out and then stared at the distant line of the dam for a long moment, hands on his hips. "It's a nice night!" he said.

A woman came down the steps, holding two cans of soda. She looked almost exactly like the man – older, overweight, with neon shorts and sandals, even what looked like the same haircut. "I brought you a pop, Henry," she said.

"Thank you kindly, Izzy," he said, taking it from her, cracking the top, and settling his bulk into a lawn chair. She took the other chair, and the two of them quietly sipped their drinks and stared out at the reservoir.

Beside me, Greta whispered, "They're just a couple of grandparents."

The man named Henry called out, "Sammy? Come on out, sit a spell!"

A lanky kid with light-brown skin and an afro appeared in the doorway. He looked like he was ten or so, dressed in jeans and a yellow T-shirt. "There are only two chairs," he said. "Where am I supposed to sit?"

"I've seen enough," Greta whispered. "They are completely harmless."

We stood and walked side by side out of the darkness.

"Hello!" Greta called, waving and smiling broadly. I copied her. We probably looked like a couple of crazies, grinning and sweeping our hands back and forth through the air like we were trying to hail a taxi.

Henry and Izzy squinted at us. Their faces were wrinkled and tanned, and I guessed they were in their late sixties. "Now what have we here?" Henry said.

"We're lost," I said.

"We were with a school group," Greta explained, "and we kind of wandered off. And then they left without us! Anyway, could we use your phone? I need to call my dad and let him know that I'm safe."

As we talked, the kid named Sammy shook his head. He looked disappointed for some reason.

A smile burst out across Izzy's face, and it was

clear where her wrinkles had come from: she probably grinned a lot. "I'll go and dig out our mobile telephone." She heaved herself up the stairs into the motor home.

Henry rubbed his chin and stared between us. "Did you two *fall in* the river? Because you look like a couple of drowned rats." He chuckled.

"We swam across the river," I said. I noticed the motor home was super shiny and new. There wasn't a scratch or a smudge on it. Not even the mud flaps were dirty.

The man stuck out his hand. "I'm Henry, my wife is Izzy, and that beanpole you see there is our nephew, Sammy. He's taken pity on a couple of old geezers and decided to spend some of his summer holiday with us."

"Hi," Sammy mumbled. And then, seeming embarrassed, he looked down at something in his lap: a handheld GameZMaster IV.

"I'm Ronan," I told them all, "and my friend's name is Greta." I didn't think it was polite to point out that summer holiday hadn't begun yet – maybe Sammy had a different set-up where he went to school.

Izzy reappeared with a smartphone. "There you go,

honey," she told Greta. "You feel free to call whoever you want. We have a good plan, so it shouldn't cost us nothing."

Greta stared at the phone, smiled tightly and said, "We're not getting a signal."

"Tell you what," Izzy said, "we only just got here and there's not so much to see that we'd be missing anything if we gave you two a lift somewheres. What say we pack up and head towards Baltimore? Once we find a signal, you can call your dad."

"We couldn't trouble you—" Greta began, but Henry cut her off.

"It's no trouble at all to help two souls in need. Besides, we want to set a good example for Sammy here." The boy rolled his eyes. "Let me put up the chairs and we'll be on the road before you can say Benedict Arnold."

Ten minutes later, we were packed into the motor home and rolling out of the car park. Henry had wedged himself into a huge caramel-coloured leather swivel chair behind the steering wheel and kept chattering non-stop about the home's HD video monitors that acted like rear-view and side-view mirrors. Behind him, Izzy was tying on an apron, standing in front of the kitchen appliances, and further back, towards the middle of the home, Greta and I were sitting with Sammy in a fake leather dining booth. He ignored us, jabbing away at the buttons on his GameZMaster IV.

The clock above the fridge said it was nearly 10 p.m. "What a crazy day," I said to Greta. I felt relaxed for the first time since my mom had come to get me at school.

Greta slouched back against the bench. "Seriously. But we're safe now."

Beside us, Sammy clucked his tongue.

Weird kid, I thought.

The motor home was kind of nice. It had everything — oven, fake fireplace, even a stacked washer/dryer, and through a door at the back was a bedroom with a full-size bed. It was like a house on wheels, if you wanted to live in the sort of place that had wall-to-wall carpeting and carpet on the walls too. Everything looked spotless and brand new. "You guys really keep this thing clean," I said.

"It even smells new," Greta said. "Did you all just buy it?"

"Sort of." Izzy smiled and turned to us, a loaf of

bread in her hands. "Have you kids had dinner yet? Why don't I make you some sandwiches?" She pulled open one drawer after another until she finally found a butter knife.

"Thanks," Greta said. "A sandwich would be great." And then she launched into some story about school in Baltimore: "We're both students there. I'm in the sciences but Ronan's more of a drama geek."

I tucked my hands in my jeans and shrugged like I was shy, because I didn't have any idea what to say – I didn't know the first thing about the drama club. I felt something hard and round in my pocket.

The purple glass disc. I'd totally forgotten to give it to Dawkins. I fished it out and turned it over a few times. It was pretty, just a few inches around and collared with a twisted strand of tarnished silver. My mom had written that it was valuable – why? Sammy watched me while his fingers moved over his GameZMaster IV. I held it to my eye and looked at him.

He stared straight back. "Nice *monocle*."

"Thanks," I said. *What a bratty kid.* "Good game?" Closing my uncovered eye, I cast my gaze around the motor home. Everything looked the same, just a lot more violet.

"It's super cool," Sammy said. "You should give it a try."

I aimed the lens towards the front of the home. "I don't thi—"

My words died in my throat.

Where Izzy stood, where Henry sat, there was nothing but the faintest of shimmers, puffs of light in the shapes of Izzy and Henry. I opened my other eye, and they were still there – Izzy singing while looking through the cupboards for plates, Henry's bulk rising up over the back of the driver's seat.

But when I closed that eye and looked again through the purple monocle, they were practically invisible. I looked at Sammy again; he was there whether I viewed him through the glass or not.

"Why don't they show up when I look at them through the purple lens?" I whispered, not meaning to speak aloud.

"Beats me," Sammy said. "Maybe there's something wrong with your monocle. But forget about that. I keep telling you, you'll be really interested in this game." He shoved the handheld across the table.

"I don't care about your video game," I said, lowering the lens. "Greta" – I pulled her into the booth and placed the monocle in her hand – "you've got to see this."

"See what?" she said, turning her attention to Sammy. "So how old are you?" she said brightly.

"I'm eleven," Sammy said in a singsong voice. "So how *dumb* are you?"

"Excuse me?" Greta said, shocked. "That's not very nice."

"Whatever," he said quietly. "I'm not one of the stupid kids who got into a motor home with two total strangers." He slid the handheld in front of her.

Written in block letters on the screen were the words TRAP THE BLOOD GUARD.

"You guys haven't even started playing," he said, "but you are already losing big-time."

CHAPTER TWELVE

THE PERFECT
FAMILY GETAWAY

Greta made a wheezing sound and dropped the monocle on to the tabletop. It tinkled and rolled around like a half-dollar until I grabbed it and stowed it back in my pocket.

"What did you just say?" Greta asked, her face white. She forced a shaky smile. "I think I misheard you."

Sammy slid around on the bench, sandwiching Greta between the two of us. "No, you heard me right," he said. "Here, I'll show you." We watched as his fingers flew over the GameZMaster IV's keys. The screen went blank and he pressed a button so that a keyboard appeared. Blindingly fast, he typed, THEY HAVE WEAPONS.

"This game is really hard to play," Greta said. She

was grey and breathing funny, like she was going to be sick.

"Be cool," Sammy whispered, popping the keyboard away. In his normal voice, he said, "So these rocker buttons control your avatar."

Three paper plates plonked down on the tabletop. "There you go," Izzy said, "a little something to tide you over until you get yourselves a proper dinner."

"Thank you *so much*," Greta said, dragging a plate towards her. "For everything. Sammy was just showing us his game."

Gazing into Izzy's face was like looking at every grandmother I'd ever met all rolled into one. She had smile lines around her eyes, just a hint of lipstick, and her cheeks were actually rosy. The people who'd killed Dawkins, who'd kidnapped my dad, they didn't look like this innocent grandma. If this sweet old lady was bad, then how would I ever know who I could trust? Evil was supposed to be obvious, wasn't it?

Trust no one, my mom had said.

"Aren't you happy to have something to eat, Ronan?" Greta asked, elbowing me.

"Yes, thank you," I said, picking up my sandwich. It was stacked high with meat and drippy with mustard.

Just the smell of it made my eyes water. "I love mustard," I lied. And then I made myself smile.

"Oh, good. Just give a holler if you want more." Izzy slowly made her way to the front of the motor home, easing into the passenger seat beside Henry.

"They shouldn't be able to hear us up there," Sammy said. He mashed his fingers against the controls.

"We have to get out of this motor home," Greta said, setting her sandwich down. To Sammy she said, "Are they really your aunt and uncle?"

Sammy scowled. "Look at me. Do I *look* related to them?" I had to admit, with his light bronze skin, dark brown eyes and loose afro, he didn't. "I only met those two last month. They're part of the same scientific society as my foster parents, but they're nobodies. Henry works at, like, a motor home showroom in Annapolis."

"But why?" Greta asked. "Why did they take the motor home and drive it up here?"

"Because of you two," he whispered, stabbing at the GameZMaster IV's buttons. "Everyone got a call and Henry got stuck going to the dam at Percy Point. Someone needed to be there in case you showed up. My foster dad made me come along. Figured you'd trust a kid over an adult."

Sammy didn't seem so bad, but I couldn't figure him out. If his foster parents were part of Ms Hand's group, like Izzy and Henry, then why would he help us? "Aren't you going to get into trouble for telling us all of this?" I asked.

"I think I'm already in trouble," Sammy said, putting the GameZMaster IV down and locking eyes with me. He looked scared. "I'm not the first kid who was fostered with the people I'm with. There was another kid in my foster family before me, right? But that kid ran away."

I couldn't understand what he was talking about. "I'm sorry, but I don't see—"

"At least, that's what they told everyone. But I'm pretty sure they were lying." He shook his head. "My fosters are part of this weird scientific movement and everybody in it is a liar. They lie straight to my face. Because I'm a kid, they think I'm stupid."

"Ronan?" Greta whispered. "She's on the phone."

Izzy was either talking to herself or had miraculously found phone reception.

Without even looking back, Sammy muttered, "She's talking to the people who sent us here, you can bet."

"Ms Hand," I said.

Sammy shrugged. "I don't know her. I only met this . . . evil guy they call the Head."

The motor home rocked and the tyres squealed. We'd made a sharp turn.

"What was that?" Greta asked loudly.

"Oh, you know what roads can be like!" Izzy said. "Lots of twists and turns."

"Don't you worry," Henry called back. "We're on our way to the interstate now."

"We need to get out of here," I whispered, standing and walking to the back. Just as I reached the bathroom, the motor home tilted as it made another hard turn.

"Sorry about that!" Henry called back. "Just taking a short cut."

I ducked inside and closed the door. The window over the toilet was too small to escape through. It was barely wide enough for me to poke my head out.

When I did, the wind outside was something fierce; wherever Henry was going, he was eager to get there. We weren't on a main road, that was for sure – the track was dirt and there were no other cars around us.

I pulled my head back in, shut the window and flushed the toilet.

The lock rattled. "Whatcha doing in there?" Izzy

called through the door.

"Using the toilet," I said. "I had to go."

"Henry said he saw your head on the rear-view cameras! Now, you're not sticking your head out of our bathroom window, are you? That would be dangerous!"

"I just . . . needed a bit of fresh air," I said. "I get car sick sometimes." I undid the bolt and opened the door.

Izzy was right there in front of me. Her friendly grandma smile had turned into a grimace – like she was about to pounce. "We can't have you putting your head out the windows, Ronan."

"I understand," I said. "I promise it won't happen again."

She seemed to relax. "Silly! Now you just go join the other kids."

"Yes, ma'am," I said, and slid in beside Greta again. Her eyes didn't seem to be focused on anything in front of her, even though Sammy kept up a non-stop patter about how to get through "Level Seven", whatever that was.

"The trick is to *escape* before the timer runs out and the game enters *lockdown*," Sammy said.

"Lockdown," I repeated.

"Yeah, it'll happen real soon. Your avatar goes through

a gate, and—"

"Why don't I make you kids another sandwich?" Izzy said from the kitchen up front.

"No, thank you," Greta said. She added, "I'm still working on this one," though neither of us had taken a bite.

Izzy reached into a drawer and pulled out the biggest butcher's knife I'd ever seen. "I'll make them better this time. I can cut the crusts off."

"You should see how big this motor home is, Greta." I said, rising and pulling her up. She hooked an arm through Dawkins' satchel as she stood. "There's even a proper bedroom in the back!"

"That is the chamber where Mr Wells and I sleep," Izzy said, chopping at the bread. "It is off limits."

I smiled and said, "We won't look at anything personal. Honest." I shoved Greta down the hall.

"That room is *private*, Evelyn, and you should heed the wishes of your elders." Izzy turned to face us, the butcher's knife held straight out.

"I really don't like—" I'd started to say automatically when I realized what she'd called me. "How do you know my first name?" I asked.

With a roar, Izzy flung the knife.

I saw everything in slow motion: Izzy's arm snapping forward; the flash of silver as the blade caught the light; her fingers wide as she let go of the handle.

I pushed Greta down and snapped open the door of the hall closet. A broom and mop tumbled out, both brand-new and wrapped in plastic.

The blade thunked hard into the closet door.

When I shut it again, the knife was sticking out of the front, its handle vibrating.

"Nice move!" Sammy said from the booth. He'd slouched down so low that he was almost completely hidden.

"You two *will* behave!" In a frenzy, Izzy yanked open a drawer, spilling silverware to the floor. The motor home tilted as it took another turn, and I was thrown against the wall. "This is why I don't like children!" she shouted.

Greta yanked me into the bedroom and slammed the door. She turned the tiny lock and stepped away. "That is not going to stop anyone," she said.

"Maybe we can block it with something," I said.

Greta yelped. "There's someone in here!"

I spun and saw shadows against the back window. Two of them. "Who are you?" I asked. But the people didn't move at all.

I slapped on the overhead light.

It revealed a smiling handsome man standing with his pretty young wife. THE PERFECT FAMILY GETAWAY VEHICLE! read a banner across their waists. They weren't real, just cardboard cut-outs for a sales display.

Greta giggled nervously, and we both stepped forward just as something shiny was thrust through the thin wood panelling of the bedroom door: the killing end of a sword.

"Open up!" Izzy shouted. The blade pivoted as she wrenched it back through the wood.

"The mattress!" I said.

We each grabbed a side and heaved it up off the bed frame. Then we wedged it tight between the floor and ceiling, blocking the entryway.

"That will slow her, like, probably three minutes," Greta said.

"Maybe it will be long enough," I said. Kicking the cardboard couple aside, I pulled the screen out of the back window. *This* one was big enough to crawl through.

Behind us, the trailer with the motorbikes rocked and bucked with each bump in the road. To our left, an aluminium ladder was bolted to the back of the motor home.

"We can go up there," I said, pointing.

"And do what?" Greta asked. "Hope they don't check the roof?"

"They'll think we leaped out the window and ran away," I said.

"No," she said, sounding tired all of a sudden, "they'll know exactly where we are. Look."

On the road behind us were headlights, faraway but closing in fast. It was a familiar-looking blood red SUV.

"They're here," Greta said.

CHAPTER THIRTEEN

A NOT-SO-GREAT ESCAPE

"The motorbikes," Greta said, pointing.

"I don't know how to ride a motorcycle," I protested, but she was already clambering out of the window and on to the ladder.

"Well, I do!" she said. Her sneakers on the bumper, she edged along until she reached the hitch where the trailer connected to the motor home.

"Be careful!" I shouted.

She scowled at me, then turned and jumped like it was no big deal, like leaping from the back of a speeding motor home on to a trailer was the sort of thing she did all the time. She landed between the two motorbikes, crouched down, and kicked at the trailer's metal tailgate until, with a bang, it fell backwards into the dirt.

"What are you waiting for?" she shouted.

She made it look so easy.

I clutched the ladder, carefully stretched my leg until my foot was firmly on a rung, then swung out of the window. "That wasn't so hard!" I shouted.

Greta just shook her head and said, "Come on!" Behind her, the tailgate dragged on the dirt road, creating a giant plume of dust that filled the air and obscured the coming headlights. If we couldn't see the people in the SUV, maybe they couldn't see us.

But apparently, Henry could, simply by looking in his rear-view cameras.

The motor home swerved left and my feet slipped. I clung to the ladder, my sneakers dangling over nothing. A moment later, Henry swerved back the other way, jerking the trailer around behind him.

The two motorbikes tumbled sideways, right on to Greta. She heaved one up, and it slid down the tailgate and vanished. The other lay on its side beneath her.

"He's trying to throw us off!" I shouted, getting my feet on the ladder again as Henry quickly jerked the motor home left and right.

Greta clung to the trailer's metal grill and waved me towards her. "Stop wasting time!" she shouted.

"I can't!" I was afraid. If Henry yanked the wheel when I jumped, I'd miss the trailer and go down on the road. But there was no reason Greta couldn't unhook the trailer and get away. "Go," I said, pointing. "The hitch!"

"OK!" Greta shouted. She pulled something from Dawkins' satchel and aimed its square nose at the hitch.

The Tesla gun.

"Wait!" I cried, scrambling up the ladder. It connected to a big metal luggage rack on the roof of the motor home. I pulled myself across it and held tight just as a bright purple sheet of light crackled up from where I'd been a moment before.

Once the afterimage cleared and I could see again, I slid to the back edge of the motor home and looked down.

"Missed!" Greta said. Still crouched on the trailer, she took aim again.

At that moment, Henry cranked the wheel so sharply that the trailer bounced and Greta fell over, her finger on the trigger.

The shot from the Tesla gun went wild, tracing a jagged arc up the back end of the motor home.

Right towards my face.

I ducked and felt the bolt sear the air over my head.

Then it swept downward again and I risked raising my head. "Stop!" I shouted. "Turn it off!"

The light disappeared as Greta released the trigger.

I peered over the edge of the motor home and gasped.

Greta had cut a five-foot-wide smoking hole in the back of the motor home, big enough for a person to climb through. Izzy screamed somewhere inside, and then a moment later, the cardboard cutouts of the family went sailing out. Greta ducked as they blew over her head and were gone.

"You put that thing down!" Izzy shouted.

Greta aimed the gun again. This time, the purple bolt found its mark, and with a giant burst of sparks, the hitch separated from the motor home.

The trailer spun sideways and away. I clutched the rack and stared helplessly into Greta's eyes as we left her behind.

I was glad she got away – I had *wanted* Greta to escape – but at the same time . . . now I was truly alone. One by one, everyone had been taken from me. My dad, my mom, then Dawkins, and now even Greta. No one was going to rescue me or tell me what to do. If I was going to be saved, I was going to have to save myself.

"OK," I said, trying to be like my mom. "Bring it on!"

Suddenly the roof of the motor home split apart like a bursting seam as a sword blade thrust up between my knees.

"Hey!" I cried, flinging myself back.

The foot of shining steel wrenched downward, only to reappear two inches in front of my face.

I scooted over to the top of the ladder, but there'd be no going down it now: Greta's wild shot with the Tesla gun had cut it almost loose except for a single bolt at the top. With every jolt of the road, it flopped and twisted in the air like a skeletal metal wing.

The noise of a car horn made me look up.

The red SUV had closed the distance and now I could make out the driver – one of Ms Hand's flunkies, probably Mr Four. Beside him was Ms Hand herself. She grinned at me and then pointed at the upper-right corner of the windscreen.

Signalling Izzy.

I scrambled the other way just as the blade poked up through the roof again.

Over the roar of the wind, I could hear Izzy's bellow – and then something else: the high-pitched whine of an engine.

A single headlight bounced towards us out of the dark, and then pulled alongside the motor home. It was Greta, astride the motorbike, her hair whipping in the wind.

She'd come back for me.

Henry must have seen her, because the motor home lurched sideways.

Greta braked and dropped back between the two vehicles, weaving back and forth to avoid the flopping ladder.

Behind her, the SUV's headlights flicked to full and it gunned forward.

They were going to ram her. I had to get off this roof now.

What would a Blood Guard do? I wondered. I flashed on a parkour class I'd taken. The teacher had us sliding down banisters all over town – until I sprained an ankle and mom declared, "That's enough of that."

"Get closer!" I shouted.

I pressed my feet against the sides of the ladder as Greta pulled alongside again, then used one leg to kick the ladder away from the motor home. As it swung up and out, I loosened my grip and slipped down its length like a fireman sliding down a pole. When I ran out of ladder, I shot out into the air—

And landed hard on the back of Greta's motorcycle, a leg on either side of the saddle. The impact knocked the breath out of me. "*Ow,*" I moaned.

"You're crazy!" Greta yelled. She rolled her wrist on the throttle and the bike shot forward.

The tyres bounced against the dirt as we left the motor home and SUV behind us. "We can go cross-country," she shouted. "They can't. So we'll just make a big loop back to the road, and then we'll follow it out of here."

But we hadn't gone all that far when we came to a twelve-foot-high chain-link fence, topped with shiny curls of razor wire. It extended from the darkness on our right and disappeared on our left.

Greta brought the bike to a halt, letting the engine idle. "I wonder if this is the lockdown Sammy mentioned," she said.

"Just cut a hole in the fence," I said. "The Tesla gun should be able to do that, no problem."

"I dropped it when the trailer came loose."

Glancing back, we could see the faraway lights of the motor home, but no sign of the SUV.

"It's OK," I said. "We can just follow the fence until we find the exit."

"Good idea," she said, popping the clutch. And just like that, we were off.

Ten minutes later, we reached the gate at the main road. It had been pulled closed, an enormous chain tightly wound through its two halves. "Can you pick that?" I asked.

Greta put down the bike's kickstand, and we both slid off and walked over to examine the padlock. "Maybe," she said. "I don't know this type of lock. It might take me a while."

Suddenly we were bathed in a bright light: the red SUV snapping on its headlights. It had been sitting silently in the dark a hundred feet away.

The doors on either side opened and I saw Mr Four aiming some kind of rifle at us. Over the other door, Ms Hand's face appeared.

Greta and I looked at one another. "We can run for—" she started to whisper before Ms Hand cut her off.

"Please," Ms Hand said. "You've caused us more than enough trouble already. I'd really rather not have to shoot you. But trust me, if I must, I will."

CHAPTER FOURTEEN

A HAND FOR A HAND

Mr Four pulled in right behind the motor home. I could see clearly through the big hole in the back that it was dark and empty.

The single-storey building in front of us was all ugly breeze block and smoked-glass windows and looked like the sort of suburban business centre where I went to the dentist every six months, only this one was plopped down in the middle of an empty scrubby field. The glass doors opened automatically when we approached, revealing a grey-carpeted lobby that was also a lot like my dentist's office. Cheap red couches sat against the walls and a flat-screen television on one wall silently played the news to the empty room.

"Come along, children," Ms Hand indicated, leading us through a door and down a hallway, flipping on light switches as she went.

The hallway was long. Lining both sides were big metal doors that were locked by simple metal bars dropped in brackets – not the sort of thing that could be opened by a girl with a lock pick.

"Here you are," Ms Hand said, dragging open the second door on her right. She ushered us inside, then slammed it shut behind us.

For a moment, Greta and I stood still in the pitch-black darkness.

The overhead lights flickered on.

Our cell was a six-foot-by-eight-foot windowless room. Fluorescent lights caged in wire mesh were fixed to the concrete ceiling, and the featureless steel door closed off any hope of escape. The only things in the room were two cots with thin, bare, yellow mattresses, and an empty bucket that I was determined not to use.

Greta sat down on one of the cots and stared at her feet. She looked completely deflated.

I sat on the other and dug the disc of glass out of my pocket. "Look," I said. "I've still got that purple monocle."

"Great," Greta said, scooting back against the wall so that her legs stuck straight out in front of her. "Maybe if you wear it, they won't recognize you when they come back."

I sighed and stuffed it back into my jeans.

"Did you get an eyeful of this place?" Greta said, her head snapping up. She wasn't depressed, I realized; she was angry. "It's where bad guys take people to kill them and dispose of the bodies so that no one ever finds any evidence."

"If they were going to kill us, don't you think they would have gotten around to it by now?" I said. If this was a place where prisoners were held, then maybe my dad was here too, in another windowless cell like this one. Maybe I could find him and rescue him myself.

"Who knows? Maybe they have to set up their evil apparatus before doing us in. Maybe they know there is no way I am going to use that bucket while you're in the room, and they're just waiting for our bladders to burst."

"You have to pee? I could look the other way."

"You'd hear."

"I can put my hands over my ears" — I demonstrated — "and sing *La la la la la la.*"

The bolt must have clicked while I had my ears covered, because the door had swung open. Ms Hand and Mr Four stood in the hallway. If they thought it was weird to see me with my hands over my ears, they didn't show it.

Ms Hand said, "Evelyn Truelove?"

"That's my name," I said with a sigh.

"Actually, he prefers to be called Ronan," Greta said. She gave me a tight little smile.

"Come with us." We both stood, but Ms Hand gestured at Greta. "You will wait here."

Out in the hall, Mr Four dropped the crossbar back into place, and then Ms Hand walked away, saying "Follow me."

At the end of the passage was a right turn and a set of double doors that Ms Hand opened by punching some numbers on a keypad. On the other side, she hit a switch and a single bar of fluorescents flickered to life.

We were in a huge dark room like the one where I'd taken Design and Technology in seventh grade. The place was packed with drill presses, table saws, lathes and other giant metal machines that stood in a shadowy row in front of a wall of floor-to-ceiling windows. In the centre of the room were two deeply scarred wooden tables, each as big as my bed at home. And sitting by itself in front of them was a simple metal folding chair.

"You guys do arts and crafts here?" I asked.

On the closer table was Dawkins' satchel, which had been cut open and was now just a mess of nylon shreds. Beside it was the Zippo lighter, Dawkins' notebook and the wad of bills. In the corner of the table sat a plastic intercom with a blinking row of lights in its base. The other table was further away, stained and dirty and empty.

"Take a seat, Evelyn." Ms Hand gestured to the chair. She looked terrible. Which made sense, I guess. She'd been hit by all that river water, tumbled around like a pair of sneakers in a washing machine. Her hair was uncombed and matted to her head on one side, her clothes a wrinkly mess.

I could see the welt on Mr Four's temple from that hubcap I'd hit him with. I hoped he wasn't the kind of guy who held a grudge.

"First," Ms Hand said after I sat, "you can save your life and that of your friend by telling us where you have hidden our property – the case in the back of our vehicle."

I thought of those evil-looking Tesla rifles in their

watery grave at the bottom of the river. Could they be dried out? Or would they be ruined? "I don't know what you're talking about," I said.

"You're lying," Ms Hand said. "But we shall see what you know soon enough." She picked up Dawkins' notebook, holding it between two fingers like it was diseased. "Now we are going to discuss the Blood Guard," she said.

"Great," I said, "I'm dying to know more about them."

"When did your mother recruit you into service?"

"She didn't," I said. "Until today, I'd never even heard of the Blood Guard."

That smile was back on Ms Hand's face, the one that made her seem like a nice mom until you got a look at her flat, dead eyes. "A reliable source informs us that your mother has been training you since you were a child."

"I guess, maybe," I said, "but she never told *me* that."

Abruptly, the smile disappeared, like a switch had been flicked off. "Joking with me is a very bad idea, Evelyn."

"I'm not joking!"

"Tell us what your mother is doing in Washington,

DC," she said, crossing her arms.

I couldn't help myself; I smiled. My mom was alive! And she was causing trouble for Ms Hand's buddies in our nation's capital. "Beats me. She didn't tell me before she kicked me out of the car."

"And your father? What do you know about him?"

Was this a trick? I thought *they* had him. Was my mom after the wrong people? Or was Ms Hand trying to find out how much I knew? "Um . . . I know you guys have him," I said, and swallowed. "He's OK, right?"

Ms Hand ignored my question. She dropped the notebook back on to the scarred wooden table, then calmly said, "Tell me about Mount Rushmore."

"It's a mountain with the faces of four presidents carved into it," I said. "George Washington, Abe Linc—"

I had never been slapped before. I had no idea it would hurt so much. It stung like my face was burning, and made my ears ring and my eyes water. I couldn't even say, "Ow." I just breathed through my open mouth and tried not to sob.

"I warned you not to make jokes," Ms Hand said. "Look at me, Evelyn."

I did as I was told. The whole left side of my face was numb.

"What does the Guard know about the Eye of the Needle?"

"You mean like the story about the camel?" I gingerly touched my cheek. It was warm. "I've never heard about anything like that."

She clucked her tongue at me. "And I suppose you know nothing about the Bend Sinister?"

I shook my head. "I don't even know what that means. Something evil?"

Ms Hand raised her open palm to hit me again, but paused when I flinched. "I almost believe you, poor thing. Raised by your mother and told nothing, forced to train for something you didn't understand at all. You should be angry with her!" She lowered her arm. "*We* are the Bend Sinister. The *sinister* in our name comes from the Latin for *left*. Not for *evil*. It is because of our foes — people like your mother — that the name of the Bend Sinister has been demonized over the centuries."

I didn't know about that. They seemed pretty evil to me. "If you say so," I said.

Ms Hand barked out a laugh, like she'd never laughed before in her life and was trying it out. Over in the corner, Mr Four stood to attention — or boredom — he was so expressionless it was hard to tell.

"The Bend Sinister is a rational society, rooted in scholarship and science," Ms Hand continued. It was sort of like a sales pitch. "We count among our members some of the greatest scientific and alchemical talents of the ages. And what binds us together? What drives us to devote our lives to the Bend Sinister? A great undertaking. A mission for good. A long-ago promise to make the world a better place."

Her words were impassioned, but she delivered them like she was reading from the world's dullest textbook. Maybe that's why I opened my big mouth. "Is that why you kill people?" I asked. "The thirty-six or whatever Dawkins called them?"

Ms Hand stopped talking and stared down at me for a long minute. Then she went over to the plastic intercom and pressed a switch. "Mr Five, Mr Two, collect the girl."

"What?" I said. "No – look, Greta's got nothing to do with any of this, honest. She's just some stupid girl from school I bumped into on the train."

"You have been lying to me since the moment you entered this room," Ms Hand said. "And because of that, your friend is going to suffer."

"But I've told you everything I know," I pleaded. "I

175

never heard of the Blood Guard before my mom told me about it yesterday afternoon, and that Dawkins guy barely had time to tell me his name before he got run over."

"Only someone who has given himself to service in the Blood Guard can do the sorts of things you've done today."

"I haven't given myself to anything! I just do as I'm told. I take a lot of extracurricular activities. I'm not even the best in my class!" I started to stand, but both Ms Hand and Mr Four tensed up, so I eased myself back down. "What is it you want from me?"

"From you? Nothing," she said. "But you'll be useful in making your mother give up the Pure One she protects. And then . . . that person will contribute his soul to our grand undertaking." Ms Hand smiled again, and for the first time since I'd met her, she seemed genuinely happy.

There were a series of beeps and a clank, and the doors opened. Greta stepped in between two guys I recognized from the train station. Mr Two and Mr Five, I guessed. They walked her over to the other wooden table. One took her arm and clasped something I hadn't noticed before over her wrist: a black metal shackle. There were four of them, I could see now – one at each corner of the table.

Greta hunched over the shackle and tugged at it. "What are they doing?"

Mr Four began rooting around in one of those giant rolling red metal toolboxes. Every now and then he'd raise up a tool – a hammer, a pair of huge clippers – and then put it back.

Mr Two and Mr Five went to the doors, punched in a code and left the room.

Greta rattled the cuff. "What's going on, Ronan?" she cried.

"How are you going to contact your mother once you reach Washington, DC, Evelyn?" Ms Hand asked.

"Until you told me, I didn't even know she was there," I said. "I was just supposed to go with Dawkins. And now he's dead. That's all I know." I couldn't allow Greta to be hurt. "Just let her go, and I'll tell you where those weapons are, the ones we took from the SUV."

"That will be a nice start, but just to show you how very serious I am, Evelyn, and to stop you from making your little jokes, we are going to have a little demonstration. Mr Four?"

177

Her partner came plodding back to her side. In one hand he held a silver hatchet, the kind you might use to chop up firewood while camping out. In the other hand he held what looked like a small black brick.

"Mr Four," she explained, "will now take your friend's hand off at the wrist."

CHAPTER FIFTEEN

HATCHET JOB

My fifth-grade summer coach, Mr Entwhistle, used to grouch that I didn't have enough "heart". Just to be clear: he coached a unicycling class, in which competing meant riding a timed course while juggling bowling pins. (As I've said before, my mom signed me up for a lot of weird courses.)

Anyway, I always figured *balance* was most important, but the coach insisted otherwise. "Something matters enough to you," he promised, "you'll reach a make-or-break point where *heart* comes in. *That's* what pushes you to do the impossible." *Make-or-break?* I thought at the time. I just didn't want to drop a pin while rounding flag fifteen.

I knew what he meant now. A cold desperation left me sweaty and breathless. I had to do *something* to save Greta. Only problem was, I had no idea what that might be. "The impossible" sounded about right.

"No!" Greta cried. She planted her heels and jerked hard at the manacle.

Mr Four set the black brick down on the corner of the table where Greta was cuffed, then began slowly dragging the blade across its surface. It was a whetstone, I realized, and he was sharpening the hatchet's edge. The light rasp of his work filled the quiet room.

"We want the cut to be clean," Ms Hand said by way of explanation.

Greta gulped. "You know, you haven't even asked *me* if I know anything. I'm happy to talk." A grin flickered across her face, like this was all a misunderstanding between friends. "I *need* my hand."

"Of course you do," Ms Hand said to Greta. "But you needn't worry. We'll let you keep it afterward. Mr Five will fetch a bucket of ice for you."

Greta didn't have any response to that. She just turned back to the shackle and yanked at it again, trying to force her hand free.

"Greta, stop," I said. "You're going to hurt yourself."

"Shut up, Ronan. It's going to hurt a lot more if they cut it off."

"That's not going to happen." I took a calming breath. "Ms Hand, the stuff about Mount Rushmore? It came out of that notebook, which belonged to Dawkins, the guy who got run over by the truck. *He's* the one you should be asking questions of."

Mr Four scraped the blade first one way, then the other. *Rasp, rasp.*

"Tsk-tsk." Ms Hand reached out and gently laid her palm against my cheek, the one she had slapped. I broke out in a sweat. "I'd like to believe you, Evelyn, truly I would. But every time I begin to do so, you reveal yourself in another lie."

"He's telling the truth!" Greta said, shaking her head so hard her hair fell over her face.

"Please, Ms Hand, don't hurt Greta. If you have to hurt someone, hurt me. Maybe that'll convince you I'm telling the truth."

The blade rasped across the whetstone half a dozen times before Ms Hand responded.

"We *will* hurt you," Ms Hand said. "But all in good time." She turned away. "Mr Four, cut off the girl's hand."

"No!" I shouted, standing.

"You need to understand, Evelyn – I am not playing." She took a step towards me. If she was angry, it didn't show. And yet somehow her icy calm was completely terrifying. "Now *sit down*."

My legs shaking, I edged back into my seat. If Dawkins were here, I knew he'd find something to use as a weapon, but all I had was the chair I was sitting on. Maybe that was enough. *I could swing it around*, I thought quickly. I could fling it hard into the air, and hit Mr Four before he—

But Mr Four and Greta were too far away, twenty feet at least. I'd never be able to take him out – not in time, not with Ms Hand between us.

Mr Four raised the hatchet, the sharp edge of its blade glimmering.

"*Please*," Greta cried, squirming and tugging at her arm.

"Be still, child," Ms Hand said. "You don't want Mr Four to slip, do you? He could easily cut off more than what's at the end of your wrist."

Greta froze, her mouth open. This was my chance.

While Ms Hand had her head turned, I stood and swung the chair up over my shoulder like a baseball bat.

Everything happened fast after that.

With the hatchet held high, Mr Four reached down with his other hand to grasp Greta's forearm, to hold her steady.

As he did, the shackle holding Greta popped open. She swept her arm up, hooked Mr Four's arm, and pulled his wrist down to where hers had been.

With a loud "Ha!" she snapped the cuff shut, locking him in, and rolled out of range as he swung at her with his hatchet. Wound around her fingers, I saw now, were two bent hairpins – *that* was why her hair had fallen across her face.

Mr Four dropped the hatchet and began moaning. He flailed against the table, jerking his whole body, trying to free himself. I just stood there like a dope, holding the chair, trying to make sense of what was going on.

Greta grabbed the hatchet and backed away.

"Mr Four!" Ms Hand shouted. "I command you to be quiet!"

Abruptly Mr Four's moans ended, though he continued to pull at his arm.

"What'd you do to him?" I asked Greta.

"Nothing!" she said.

"He. . ." Ms Hand seemed at a loss for words. "The flesh is all he has left. It dislikes confinement."

Flesh? I thought. *Confinement?* I had no idea what she was talking about, but that was nothing new. "Just stay where you are," I told Ms Hand. "I'm not afraid to . . . use this chair."

Ms Hand scoffed. "You think you're in control? Because the girl slipped out of a simple handcuff?" She straightened her jacket.

"*Simple* handcuff?" Greta repeated. "That was like a six-pin tumbler." She tipped her chin up. "Not a challenge for me obviously. I could pick it in my sleep."

"OK, Houdini," I said, "you're the master locksmith. Can we just go now?"

Ms Hand took a step forward, but paused when Greta swung the hatchet in the air. "Careful with that, child. You don't want to hurt yourself."

Greta snorted. "Your concern for my well-being is touching." With a roll of her wrist, she flipped the hatchet into the air. It spun a tight loop and she caught it by the handle. Without looking away from Ms Hand, she brought the blade down to her right – straight across the intercom line. The little lights in the base went dark.

"You know how to use hatchets too?" I asked as we backed away.

"And axes," Greta said. "My dad's an outdoorsman. You think you're the only one who's ever gone camping?"

"You are outnumbered," Ms Hand said. She didn't appear in the least bit alarmed by our escape. "Mr Two and Mr Five are outside, as well as the two acolytes and that boy."

"Acolytes?" Greta asked.

"I think she means Izzy and Henry," I said.

"They will kill you," Ms Hand said.

"We'll take our chances," I replied. I pocketed Dawkins' notebook, the money and the Zippo lighter. "What's the code for the door?"

Ms Hand put her arms behind her back. "Do you really think I'm going to tell you that?"

"We could always take a page from your book and cut off Mr Four's hand," I said.

"And you pretend you know nothing of the Blood Guard." Ms Hand muttered something under her breath, a quiet singsong.

"I don't," I said. "Why won't you believe me?" That's when I caught the reflection in the windows: her hands were beginning to glow. "Cut that out!" I shouted, and raised the chair, ready to fling it. "Stop casting a spell or whatever you're doing!"

But she didn't stop, only brought her arms out where we could see them. The space around her hands shimmered with a red light.

"It's OK, Ronan," Greta said. She punched the keypad and the door unlocked. "Those two guys didn't bother to block my view when they brought me in here."

Ms Hand's cool composure fell away and she raised her glowing hands. "Mr Two!" she yelled, her eyes angry slits. "Mr Five! Come to me!"

But the hall was empty.

Greta turned the hatchet in her hand and brought the blunt end down hard on the keypad. The face popped off its housing and dangled from a bunch of sparking wires.

"You will not—" Ms Hand began to say, but by that point we were on the other side of the door and pulling it closed behind us. The lock clicked into place, and Greta repeated her move on the outside keypad until it too was a mess of broken hardware.

It was dark in the hall. The only illumination came from a flickering, buzzing light somewhere around the corner.

"Just to be clear," Greta whispered while we waited for our eyes to adjust to the dark, "I am not cutting *anything* off *anyone*."

"*I* know that," I said. "I'm just glad *she* didn't."

Behind us, the door shuddered in its frame. Ms Hand sang something, and the metal of the door slowly began to buckle outward with a deep groan.

"We should get out of here," Greta said.

"I wonder where those other two guys are," I said.

She eyeballed the metal chair I was still holding. "What are you going to do with that? Invite them to have a seat?"

I hefted it up. "What else have I got?"

Greta looked ready to say something more, then held a finger to her lips. "Someone's coming," she whispered.

I held my breath and could hear light footsteps in the corridor. The ratchet of a cell door being opened, then eased shut. Footsteps again, coming closer. Another cell door opened. Periodically a spot of light would dance along the wall — a torch beam.

"Maybe they caught more prisoners?" I whispered, thinking of my mom and dad.

Greta's eyebrows rose. Pushing her hair behind her ears, she raised the hatchet up — still backwards, blunt end first.

"No," I said, raising the chair over my right shoulder. "I'll hit them with this and knock 'em down. And then we can go for their weapons."

I quietly edged along the wall towards the corner.

The torch's beam grew brighter. We could hear whoever it was breathing as he shut the last door and walked towards the end of the hall.

Behind us, Ms Hand let loose on the door with another spell of some sort – the metal that had buckled outward now shimmered and bent inward. But the door still held.

The footsteps paused, then started again, but more quietly. Whoever it was had heard her and changed his gait.

"Now!" Greta hissed.

We stepped around the corner and I swung the chair as hard as I could.

It connected with a muffled clang – the sound of a steel chair thudding into a human torso.

"Ow!" someone said, falling back in a heap. The torch clattered to the floor and rolled away. "What the dickens did you hit me with?"

I brandished the chair at the shadowy figure on the floor and said, "Don't even think of getting up."

"I've got a hatchet," Greta added, "and I know how to use it." With her left hand, she felt along the wall until she found the light switch, then flipped it on.

Lying on the floor was Jack Dawkins.

CHAPTER SIXTEEN

NEVER SAY DIE

"What'd you go and hit me for?" He glared at us while hugging his arms around his middle. "And with a *chair*? What sort of brute uses a *chair*?"

"Dawkins?" Greta squeaked, her voice catching in her throat. "Dawkins!" She dropped the hatchet and dived forward to hug him. "You're alive!"

"Mind the ribs," he said, wincing. "Still a bit tender."

"But you were dead," I insisted. We'd seen his arm sticking out from beneath a couple tons of lorry. People don't just get up and walk away from things like that.

"And yet here I am." Dawkins dragged his hands

down the front of his dirty T-shirt. There were new stains on it – what looked like blood and oil, and one that was obviously the mark from an enormous tyre tread – but he looked much the same. He got to his feet, stretched his neck to work out a kink, then bent and picked up the torch. "Dead, Ronan? Dead is just a state of mind."

"I'm pretty sure that dead is more than just a state of mind," Greta said. "You were *smushed*." She hugged him again. It was like by dying and coming back to life, he'd become her favourite person in the world.

"It was a wee tiny truck—"

"It was a *huge* truck. It was horrible." Greta's face crumpled up. "Your hand was sticking out from under the tyres, all like, *Aaagh!*"

"How do you even know that was me?"

"You were wearing that." I pointed to the dirty brown leather jacket. "The one you still have on. The one with blood all over it. And tread marks."

"Fine, you're right; I'm a proper mess." He looked down and sighed. "I wish we had time for me to have a wash and explain, but that will have to wait, I'm afraid. Right now we are in a bit of a hurry."

From inside the room, Ms Hand let loose with another

spell, and this time the metal in the door wavered as if it were starting to melt. Dawkins aimed the beam of the torch at it, then at the dangling keypad. "Whoever is in there seems pretty keen to get out."

"It's the woman who's been chasing us," I said. "The one from the truck stop. Ms Hand. We locked her and one of her helpers inside."

"You two did this?" Dawkins said, beaming. "Now that is *strong work*! I'm impressed. My chest would swell with pride if only it didn't hurt so much."

"Sorry about the chair," I said.

"Oh, it was more that business with the truck," he replied. "Takes a while for me to get back to a hundred per cent." He shrugged. "But enough jibber-jabber! Let's get a move on."

I picked up my chair.

"Are you kidding?" Greta said to me. "Leave it."

"No way. I feel defenceless without it."

"It's a *chair*."

"It hurt Dawkins, didn't it?"

Dawkins said, "He's got a point there." He turned back down the hall towards the entrance and we fell in behind him.

"How did you get here?" Greta asked.

"I don't rightly know," he said. "Once I came to, I discovered myself snugged up tight in a giant plastic bag. That was a first."

"Yeah," I said. "They'd gone and picked up – well, your body. If you'd been dead, I mean. But if you were alive, then I guess it was—"

"Still my body. I just happened to be not quite done using it."

"Right. They grabbed your body and the other guy's," I said, beginning to put it all together. Someone must have moved the body bags from the back of the SUV into the compound. "But why did they take the bodies in the first place?"

"They were likely planning to interrogate me if I came back to myself, so to speak," Dawkins said. "They know that Overseers are, um, especially durable."

"But you were *smushed*," Greta said again.

"So you keep telling me," he said. We'd reached the door to the lobby. "At any rate, body bags are not like sleeping bags – they don't put zippers on the inside. Who knew?" Dawkins pressed his ear against the door. "Peaceful as a tomb," he said, easing it open.

Lying face down on the carpet of the lobby were Izzy and Henry. Both had their hands tied behind their backs, their feet bound together and socks balled up in their mouths. Izzy glared at us, a bruise blooming over her left eye.

"Do you know these two grey-haired hooligans?" Dawkins asked, gesturing.

"Unfortunately," Greta said. "Who tied them up?"

Dawkins gave a bow. "My handiwork. They weren't being very friendly and so. . . Where was I? Right: zipped tight into this body bag, and I didn't know where I was – I figured a morgue of some sort. I couldn't get out and I didn't have any kind of blade on me, so I did what anyone would do: I started hopping around and shouting, 'Hello! Hello!'"

"You were still in the body bag?" I asked.

"What do you not understand about my being unable to free myself from that thing?" He nodded towards Izzy. "That tubby old viper there came and unzipped me. I could tell from the Tesla gun she held that she was no friend of mine, so I did what comes naturally." He tapped his temple. "I head-butted her."

Izzy growled something and Dawkins snapped, "I apologized already. Now, which of you has the keys to that motor home out there?" Her eyes flicked to Henry, and Dawkins said, "Old Man Winter, eh?" He patted Henry's pockets and found the keys, then said, "OK, kids, I think we should take this reunion on the road."

"What about Sammy?" Greta said.

"Who?" Dawkins said.

"This kid who was travelling with these two," I explained, glancing around. There was another door out of the lobby, one I hadn't noticed when we'd first arrived. "He saved us when we were in the motor home."

"If he saved you," Dawkins asked, "what are you doing *here*?"

"OK, he *tried* to save us, but we got caught anyway," Greta said. "Maybe he's locked up here too. We've got to help him."

Dawkins rolled his shoulders until something popped, then stood up straighter. "What's one more kid? I swear, I've become a glorified babysitter. Let's go find this Sammy character."

Dawkins opened the door off the lobby and we followed him into a small room with a wall of grey metal lockers and two wooden benches. Facing us was a gun rack loaded with rifles – ordinary ones without the Tesla modifications. Next to the rifles was a fat duffel bag.

"We'd best find something with which to defend ourselves," Dawkins said. He opened the duffel and peered inside. "These will do." He took out two sheathed swords that curved slightly at the tips, then drew them from their scabbards. "Briquet sabres, Napoleonic era. A bit unwieldy, and fancier than I generally go for, but we don't really have a choice."

"Why don't we just use the guns?" I asked.

Dawkins crossed and uncrossed the sabres a few times, and a whisper of metal filled the room. "Guns are dishonourable."

"Hard to be honourable when the other guy brings a gun to a knife fight," Greta said.

"Not when the person wielding the knife is one of the Blood Guard. We can – well, slow down time itself. A Guard's reactions are fast enough to mark a bullet's trajectory and deflect it. So guns are, for the most part, ineffective against us." In my mind's eye I saw my mom charging the fake cops in Stanhope, knocking aside their bullets with her cutlass. And I remembered the paddle I'd used on the river. But what I did wasn't the same thing, was it?

A sword in each fist, Dawkins sidled up to a swinging door on the opposite wall of the dressing room. "Now let's see what's on the other side of this."

"What about us?" Greta said. "Shouldn't we have something to defend ourselves?"

"You mean a *weapon*?" he said, his voice dripping disbelief. "You two are practically *children*; you could get hurt." He tipped his chin at me. "Besides, Ronan has his chair. If we run into any trouble, he can sit on our foes."

"Can we just find Sammy and get out of here?" I asked. "That locked door isn't going to hold Ms Hand much longer."

"Right, then," Dawkins said. He backed into the door, turning as he did. We followed.

Beyond was another hall like the one we'd come from – a similar row of cell doors, the same fluorescent lights, the same tan tiles on the floor. But coming around the corner at the far end were the two men who'd brought Greta to Ms Hand – Mr Two and Mr Five. They skidded to a stop as the door swished back and forth behind us with a soft *fwap-fwap-fwap*.

"Hello, there!" Dawkins called, walking down the hall to meet them.

Mr Two and Mr Five both held Tesla rifles. Clearly the ones we'd disposed of weren't the only Tesla weapons these people had.

"I really wouldn't shoot those newfangled gadgets in here, if I were you. Who knows what's in these pipes overhead." Dawkins gestured with one of his sabres. "Could be extraordinarily messy."

They levelled their rifles.

"Duck!" Dawkins shouted as they opened fire.

He took three enormous leaping strides, then dropped to his knees and slid. As he did, he spun the swords in swift, short arcs, catching the violet Tesla bolts with the flats of his blades. The beams ricocheted off the swords into the walls and ceiling, shattering the lights and the bulb housings and showering glass and metal down on everything.

And then the bolts seemed to fuse, and I realized that Dawkins wasn't just blocking the beams. He was aiming them, reflecting them away from himself and back at the two men.

Startled, Mr Two and Mr Five released the triggers.

Dawkins rolled a neat somersault and planted his feet on the ground, then exploded into the air, sailing high, right between the two men.

Mr Two dodged out of reach, but Mr Five wasn't as fast, and Dawkins swung the hilt of one sword hard against his temple. The man crumpled to the floor.

Dawkins bounced off the far wall to the ground.

It took him only a moment to get back on his feet, but that was long enough for Mr Two to take aim at Greta and fire off a shot from his Tesla rifle.

Greta was as good as dead. Except. . .

Nothing is as fast as the speed of light, but somehow that split second lasted a short eternity. There was Mr Two, grimacing as he squeezed the trigger. Behind him, Dawkins already springing into the air again, bringing up his swords. Greta, one hand on the wall of the corridor, slowly – way too slowly – dropping to the floor, trying to get out of the way.

And somehow, interrupting it all, my stupid metal chair.

When had I thrown it? I don't know.

It looked almost weightless, tumbling gently end over end, spinning up right in front of Greta before the Tesla bolt struck her.

The chair didn't explode – not quite – but the discharge from the Tesla gun caught it full-on, and it burst into bright light. I squeezed my eyes shut, but I could still see the outline in the dark, as though its shape had been traced by laser beams.

A smouldering shower of steel pattered to the floor

around us. A few bits landed in Greta's hair but I swatted them out. A thin electrical stink filled the air.

From down the hall someone grunted, "Unh!" and then the searing light from the Tesla gun was gone and Dawkins was standing over the two unconscious Bend Sinister agents.

"Wow," Greta gasped.

"What did I just do?" I whispered.

"Saved my life," she said. I reached out a hand and pulled her up, and then she hugged me, hard enough that I wheezed. "Thank you," she whispered.

"I *knew* Ronan's chair would come in handy!" Dawkins hollered from the other end of the hall. "I'll make a Blood Guard of you yet, Ronan Truelove."

The big room around the corner was the mirror image of the one where Ms Hand had interviewed me — scarred wooden tables, the same cold concrete floor, even the same pass code to open the door. But there was no sign of Sammy. "That's a relief," Greta said, rubbing her wrist. "I was afraid we might find him — or his hand — on one of those tables."

Instead, there was a map and a blueprint, the kind architects use. Dawkins scanned both, said, "Don't mind if I do," then folded them up. I remembered that I had his notebook and wordlessly handed it to him. He nodded and tucked everything into his jacket.

Next, we checked each of the cells in the long corridor. Midway down, we found what we were looking for: Sammy.

He was stretched out on a cot, focused on his GameZMaster IV. He flinched a little when the door opened, then slowly relaxed when he saw it was us. "I thought you guys might be someone else," he said, his eyes searching the hall behind us. "Izzy told me the Head guy was going to punish me for helping you, but I told her she had it wrong. You figured out what was going on with them all by yourself, right? Maybe if you told her, she'd believe you."

"You don't have to worry about them," Greta said.

"We're busting you out," I said. "Taking you to safety."

"That's good," Sammy said, but he still looked anxious. He pointed at Dawkins. "Who's he?"

"A friend," Greta said. "His name is Jack Dawkins."

"You're sure he's not one of them?" Sammy's grin twitched, and I realized just how terrified he was.

"No way," I assured him. "Dawkins is on our side."

Sammy shoved his GameZMaster IV under one arm and stretched out his right hand. "In that case," he said, dead serious, "I am very happy to meet you."

CHAPTER SEVENTEEN

THE SOUL OF THE MATTER

In the car park, Dawkins neatly stabbed each of the tyres of the two red SUVs. The air filled with a loud hissing. "That should slow them down a bit," he said.

Then he came around the motor home and saw the hole Greta had carved into the back. Some of the wiring near the upper right-hand corner was still spitting out an occasional spark. "What happened here?"

"Greta was trying to get the trailer free, but we couldn't get the hitch loose, and Izzy was chopping at us with a sword and so Greta had to use a Tesla gun to cut off—"

"Never mind," Dawkins said. "I just wish one of you had mentioned that the motor home lacked a proper back end *before* I ruined the other means of transport here." We all looked at the SUVs, now resting on their flattened tyres. He sighed and waved us aboard. "I only hope there's something to eat in here."

He stowed the swords in the motor home's closet, then slid behind the wheel and cranked the ignition. As he wrestled the vehicle down the road, he tapped the bank of small screens set in the dashboard. "Sammy, I assume one of these is a GPS mapping thingamajig?"

"That one," Sammy said. "You type in the address and it shows which way to go. The other three are for the rear-view cameras." He pushed a switch and the screens glowed.

"Will those people be able to track us?" Greta asked.

"Doubtless," Dawkins said. "But my hope is that we can outrun them and get to DC before they wise up to our escape."

"We're going to DC again?" I asked. "Not Roanoke?"

"Our plans have changed again, Ronan," he said, shivering so hard his hands shook on the wheel. "There are events under way that we need to stop. Even if doing so means exposing some of the Blood Guard and risking retaliation."

"DC sounds good to me," Greta said. "I really need to see my dad."

Dawkins cast a sidelong glance at her. "Right," he said. "That's a good idea."

"And we can meet up with my mum," I said, and told them what Ms Hand had revealed.

Suddenly, looming up ahead of us in the headlights, were the locked chain-link gates, with Greta's motorbike still parked in front of them.

"I can go and move the—" I started to say.

"Do you jest?" Dawkins said, stomping on the accelerator. "We are not stopping again until we reach DC."

He swerved the motor home around the bike and straight through the gates. They burst open, the chain snapping like it wasn't even there.

"That. Was. Awesome," Sammy declared, whistling.

"That's nothing," Dawkins said, typing an address into the GPS unit. "If you really want to see awesome, make me a sandwich."

"There was some bread and stuff back there," I said, walking to the kitchenette. "I'll see what I can find."

The cupboards were filled with a random assortment of groceries – two cans of soup, a bag of coffee, a package of straws. Straight off the showroom floor, I remembered. Above the sink I found a jar of peanut butter and the loaf of bread. I picked a butter knife up off the floor and washed it in the sink.

"Sammy, tell me how you came to be mixed up with these people," Dawkins said, cracking open the driver's side window an inch. A cool breeze blew down the length of the motor home and out the giant hole in the back.

I looked down the road behind us, fearing I'd see headlights – Ms Hand and her glassy-eyed, numbered flunkies, but there was nothing. I sighed with relief and got to work making a sandwich.

"My foster parents," Sammy said. "They're scientists. And they belong to this big association of other scientists who are all working on a super-important project." He got quiet. "My mom died a couple years ago and I didn't have anyone else. I've been in, like, four foster homes. This one seemed OK at first."

"Ms Hand talked about a scientific society," I said. "She said they were doing 'a great undertaking'."

"We need a lot less talking and a lot more sandwich-making, Ronan," Dawkins called back. "That whole coming-back-from-an-early-grave bit? That spot of rescuing I did back there? Those heroic deeds require *a lot* of energy, and energy requires fuel." When no one responded, he added, "And by fuel, I mean *food*."

The mud track ended at a stretch of asphalt: a two-lane highway, the dashed yellow lines luminous in the glow of the headlights. I didn't think I'd ever been so happy to see something so ordinary. Without a word, Dawkins turned left and took us up to the speed limit.

I set the sandwich on a paper plate and started back to the front. But before I'd taken two steps, Dawkins said, "Not so fast. You've seen me eat. Turn that *entire* loaf into sandwiches, if you please."

Greta found another knife, and said, "I'll help."

"They seemed OK at first?" Dawkins asked Sammy.

"I'm not the first foster kid who lived with the Warners. The girl before me ran away. That's what they told me, but I think something else happened. I found her diary behind the dresser. What kid runs away and doesn't take her diary with her?"

"Just because she left her diary doesn't mean they did something to her," Greta said.

"I know that! But the stuff she wrote about was. . ." Sammy looked down at his hands, and I remembered that he was only eleven. "They were doing experiments, and the Head guy would put on this freaky three-eyed mask to examine her. She wrote that the mask was *alive*. It moved."

"Creepy!" Greta said, pausing with a wad of peanut butter balanced on her knife.

"The mask was some kind of creature?" I asked.

"Only when it was on his face, I guess. After she described that, the diary just ended," Sammy said. "Something bad happened to her, I bet, and it's because of the Head guy in the mask."

"Did you catch this Head guy's name?" Dawkins asked. "That would help."

"I think I heard it once, but . . . that was before I'd found the diary. I wasn't really paying attention." Sammy sighed and sank into the seat. "Mostly they just call him the Head. He's this middle-aged guy in a business suit who looks normal and pretends to be nice, but you can tell he's just sizing you up. He is cold, cold, cold."

Dawkins drove silently for a moment. "Tell me, Sammy, what exactly do your foster parents do?"

"They're particle physicists. Dr Warner – that's my foster dad – publishes articles with weird titles like 'The SubAtomic Smoke Trail of the Soul'. My foster mom works as a scientist too." He swivelled his chair and stared into the dark outside the window. "I don't really see them all that much, to be honest. They're always in the lab."

"My dad is the same," I said. "Some weekends I forget he's even part of the family." These past few years, he was always working, always travelling, and I couldn't even tell you what he wore on any given day, because most days I didn't see him at all. I swore to myself that was going to change after today. Once my mom and I rescued him, we'd be a family again.

"Speak for yourself," Greta said. "My parents aren't like that. I see my mom all the time. My dad too."

"Ronan, Greta, seriously – I am in dire need of sustenance." Dawkins' eyes caught mine in the rear-view mirror. They were dark-ringed and exhausted-looking. He'd been run over by a lorry, I reminded myself. "Where's the chow?"

Greta stacked the plate high with sandwiches and came forward. "Right here."

"Just drop those in my lap. I can take care of the rest." Dawkins scooped up a sandwich, wadded it up with his right hand, and began stuffing it into his face. "Your foster parents?" he asked, his mouth full. "Those were the two oldsters we left tied up in the lobby of that building?"

"No, no – that's Izzy and Henry. They're what my foster mom calls *acolytes*. They do odd jobs at the lab and just hang around. When the alarm came in about you guys, they volunteered. Dr Warner called me and told me I had a role to play. He figured Greta and Ronan might not trust two strange old people, but that kids would trust a kid."

"It's true," I said. "Izzy and Henry did seem a lot less obviously weird because you were there."

"Still weird," Greta agreed, "just not as *obviously* weird."

"Oh, they're the weirdest." Sammy nodded.

"What I don't understand is why they want you so bad, Ronan," Greta asked.

"Ms Hand told me she wanted to use me to get at my mom," I said, "but that wasn't all."

Dawkins folded a sandwich into his mouth. "What else?"

"She asked me about the Eye of the Needle," I said.

"Matthew 19:24," Dawkins explained. "That's the whole 'easier for a camel to go through the eye of a needle, than for a rich man to enter the kingdom of God' business."

"Mrs Warner said the same thing," Sammy said, "when I asked her about what it meant. She'd written it across the top of a diagram that I found on the kitchen table."

"And she probably wasn't checking to see that you'd done your Sunday school reading." Dawkins nibbled at a sandwich instead of swallowing it whole. "I don't like how this is all fitting together."

"How is it fitting together?" Greta asked.

"What was that diagram of?" Dawkins asked Sammy, ignoring Greta's question.

"I'm not sure. It looked like a big basketball hoop." Sammy made a circle in the air with his hands. "It even had a net and stuff."

"Maybe it actually *was* a basketball hoop," I said.

"Sure," Greta said. "This Head guy hires Sammy's parents — who are physicists — to make basketball hoops for them. Because he's going to field a team in the NBA."

"Put that way, it doesn't sound so likely," I said.

"This isn't good," Dawkins muttered. "This isn't good at all." He bolted down another sandwich, but he didn't look happy.

"Why?" I asked. "What is it a diagram of?"

"I don't know," Dawkins said, "but I have my

suspicions. Hearing what Sammy's parents are working on; hearing about this Eye of the Needle. . ." He finished the last sandwich in two big bites. "The situation is far worse than any of us thought."

"They've taken my dad and kidnapped us, and they almost cut off Greta's hand," I said. "How much worse can it be?"

"You have no idea." Dawkins glanced over his shoulder at me, but he seemed to be looking further — through the hole in the motor home, across the darkness behind us and back to the building, where Ms Hand and her team were up to no good. "It appears they've solved a puzzle they've been struggling with for centuries and now can do what should be impossible."

"And what is that?" I asked.

"Oh, nothing much, Evelyn Ronan Truelove," Dawkins said. "But it appears that they've found a way to trap the human soul."

CHAPTER EIGHTEEN

WAITING FOR THE
END OF THE WORLD

Sammy's eyes bulged as he gaped at Dawkins and then me, his jaw wide open. "Your name is Evelyn *Truelove*?"

"It's a pretty silly name, I know," I said. "Just call me Ronan."

"No one cares about your stupid name," Greta muttered, but Sammy blinked at me like I'd grown horns.

"You OK?" I asked him.

"I think I'm just tired," he said, covering his face and letting out a giant yawn. "Is it OK if I go to sleep?"

"Absolutely," Dawkins said. "Though I fear the back bedroom may be a bit windy."

Sammy stumbled past us to the dining nook, where he curled up on one of the padded benches.

Poor kid, I thought, picturing Izzy and Henry. "I'm beat too," I said, sliding into the empty passenger seat.

"I'll sleep later," Greta said. "I want to know why these people want to trap souls."

Dawkins sighed. "I suppose there's no harm in telling you two everything, seeing as you're already hip-deep in this. That scientific society Sammy's foster parents joined? It's a centuries-old group who are working hard to bring about the end of the world."

"Why would anybody want to do that?" I asked.

"Because they can?" Dawkins said, shrugging. "Why does anyone do anything? They believe humanity is rotten with sin, and the only way to save the Earth is to scour it clean with a hellfire that rids the planet of everyone but themselves. Like Noah's ark, only with fire this time."

"So they want to start again," Greta said. "Except this time the survivors will be the bad guys."

"Not in their eyes," Dawkins said. "They believe they're the *good* guys — the only ones with the courage to do the hard work required to save the world."

I thought of Ms Hand lecturing me. "The Bend Sinister," I said.

Dawkins lifted an eyebrow. "That's their name. They

fancy themselves scholars and scientists, but it's all just window-dressing for run-of-the-mill evil. Instead of working to make the world a better place, they're dedicated to trying to kill the thirty-six Pure. That is the whole reason the Bend Sinister exists: to murder people, and in so doing, bring about the end times."

"What's a Pure?" Greta asked.

But Dawkins was on a roll. He ignored her question and just kept talking. "And yet they've never succeeded. Why? Because" – he raised his thumb – "one: they don't know who the thirty-six *are*. Sometimes they uncover the identity of, at best, a few, but they've never managed to murder more than five at once. Which can plunge the world into a whole mess of trouble, but doesn't quite bring about the end."

"And reason number two," I said, thinking of my mom, "is that the Blood Guard are there, protecting the thirty-six."

"Exactly," Dawkins said, leaning back in the seat. "We Guards devote ourselves to making sure the Pure One's life is as regular and boring as can be. Ideally they live lives of unspoiled grace and then die a natural death.

"But nonetheless, the unexpected sometimes happens. The Bend uncovers a Pure's identity, defeats the Guard and kills the person we swore to protect. The world becomes a darker place, but only until the preordained time for that soul to be reincarnated. Eventually it returns to the world in a new vessel, a new person whose birth tips the scales back into balance."

"But if the soul doesn't reincarnate?" I asked, thinking about this Eye of the Needle device. "If it gets trapped?"

"That, my friend, is the crux of the problem." Dawkins shook his fist. "Souls are *not* supposed to be something you can trap, not something you can pluck out of a body with a pair of magical tweezers. Souls return." For the first time in our short acquaintance, Dawkins' voice sounded full of heartache. "They *always* return. That's the final safeguard."

"Until now?" I asked.

"So it appears." He steered the motor home into the southbound lane of a broad freeway, four lanes in each direction, light traffic on both sides. Through the windscreen, the lights of a city glowed on the horizon. The clock on the dashboard said it was well past two in the morning.

"*If* the Bend can stop the souls of the Pure from reincarnating, they need only trap a soul and hold on to it. Eventually, they will have stopped enough of the Pure from coming back into the world. And then. . ."

"And then. . . ?" Greta asked so softly that I could barely hear her.

"And then the world will end," Dawkins said, tightening his hands on the steering wheel.

There was nothing to say to that, so we just looked out at the road and the darkness that seemed to swallow up the world around us. Our silence lasted long enough that I started getting antsy. I needed to hear something – anything – even if it was only my own voice.

"Hey!" I said, my voice louder than I'd intended. "I never told you about the purple monocle my mom gave me—"

"She gave the Verity Glass to *you*?" Dawkins said, shaking his head. "Awfully trusting."

"Maybe not so much," I said, thinking of what my mom had written on the envelope. "I was supposed to give it to whoever I met on the train. You, I guess."

"Please tell me that the Bend Sinister didn't find it and take it from you," Dawkins said, his eyes glancing off Greta before meeting my own.

"No," I said, patting my jeans. "I've got it right here. You want it?"

"Just keep it in your pocket for now," he said with a shake of his head.

"It was strange," I went on. "When I used it to look at Izzy and Henry, those people from the motor home, they were just kind of shimmery outlines."

"That's because they're not there in a way the Verity Glass can see. They've signed over their life force to further the cause. Many Bend Sinister acolytes donate their animating spark, that spiritual essence that carries a person through his or her life.

"All that sacrificed life force adds up to a mighty raw power. It's channelled by the Hands."

"Like Ms Hand?" Greta asked.

Dawkins scowled. "That's her title, not her name. A Hand can use the power herself or funnel it through her minions, that bunch of soulless brutes who tag along in her wake."

"Back at the safe house," I said, "when Greta trapped Mr Four, Ms Hand said—"

"'The flesh is all he has left'," Greta said.

"Your Mr Four barely exists now except as an extension of the so-called Ms Hand. But through him and others like him, she can perform wondrous feats."

"We saw some of that," I said, and told him about

Mr Four at the river.

"But worse even than the Hands," Dawkins continued, "are the Heads. No one knows their identities. Who are they when they're not bent on evil? We have no idea. They pretend to be ordinary people, holding down ordinary jobs. The Blood Guard's work would be tons simpler if the Heads would just, I don't know, wear some kind of universally recognized sign of wickedness."

"What about that tattoo," I said, "the open eye with the wavy lines coming off it? Couldn't you look for that?"

"The symbol of the Perceptor," Dawkins said. "An all-seeing eye before which nothing can be hidden. That girl's diary Sammy mentioned? She'd been examined by the Perceptor. It's sort of like a Verity Glass, except it's a sickly green and glows, and the Bend Sinister mount it in this horrifying mask."

"You drew a picture of it!" Greta said. "In your notebook."

Dawkins nodded. "I've never seen one myself, but that's what I'm told it looks like. It allows the user to actually *perceive* souls, but it's supposed to have other abilities as well. The tattoo of the Perceptor, however, is not for anyone who must move unrecognized in the world. So a Head wouldn't be marked."

"Are you one of those Pures you mentioned?" Greta asked, resting her hand on Dawkins' shoulder. "Were you reincarnated? After the truck stop?"

Dawkins laughed. "Afraid not! That was just plain old healing. An Overseer's body repairs itself no matter what befalls it. That's why I eat so much – I have a metabolism like a furnace."

"You healed?" I asked. "An articulated lorry comes to a stop on top of you and you just . . . get better?"

"Yes, Ronan, I heal. Very quickly, perhaps, but just like your body does when you have a cut or a broken bone. Overseers cannot be killed. *Nunquam mori*, it's called by the Guard, which is just a fussy way of saying 'Never die' in Latin. I've hidden my death, and as a result, the world is stuck with me until I decide to shuffle off."

"I wish I could do that," I said, and thought of my mom. "Are all Blood Guards immortal?"

"No, only the Overseers," Dawkins said. "And trust me, you do *not* wish it for yourself or anyone you love. It *hurts*. Though I may not be able to be killed, I still feel every almost-death." His whole body shivered. "Nausea and pain so overwhelming that a real death would be a mercy. But then" – he caught my eye – "as you say, I get better."

"So does this mean you've been alive a long time?" Greta asked.

"A couple of hundred years, though I am relatively young in the ranks of the Blood Guard's Overseers."

"You're two hundred years old?"

"Not quite," Dawkins said, "but another ten years or so and. . ."

"That means you were born in . . . 1824?" Greta said.

"1821, actually. It was about ten years later that I got involved with the Blood Guard, though I didn't understand that at the time. At first all I understood was that I'd picked the wrong pocket."

"So you've been a thief all your life," Greta said.

"Pickpocket," he corrected her. "There's a difference. Picking pockets takes . . . art. Prestidigitation. Finesse. Thieving is just smash and grab."

"Stealing is stealing." Greta folded her legs against her chest and wrapped her arms around them, then closed her eyes. "Where was this again?" she asked with a yawn.

"England," Dawkins said. "I was born the month

Napoleon Bonaparte died, May of 1821. I came into the world in a dark little hole of a town called Northampton, within an even darker, smaller hole called a workhouse.

"My mum had gone there when no other place would have her; she was poor, pregnant, without a husband or a job. A few years later, she finally got out, sewn into a burlap sack and tossed in a potter's field with a shovelful of lime, lost among all the others who'd died in the workhouses.

"Not being the trusting sort, I ran away at the first chance I got, just after I turned eight. My feet carried me south to London and into the company of two similarly homeless children named Agatha and Spinks. We were scavengers and thieves and always hungry. One winter when I was ten or so, we spotted the perfect target. . ."

CHAPTER NINETEEN

JACK DAWKINS,
FISHER OF WALLETS

We pegged her the moment she glided into the new market square at Covent Garden. She was large and soft and pale, and wrapped up in a blood-red silk brocade day dress that whispered *money*.

"Pretty," Agatha whispered, clutching her ragged coat.

"Pretty easy target, you mean," Spinks said.

Staying back a few yards, we followed her down the aisle between the stalls, snaking through the crooked tumble of carts and booths, and not stopping long enough to catch anyone's ire.

The vendors sold everything you could ever want and a lot more besides. There were bakers, butchers and fishmongers; men selling chicken, pigeon and duck; greengrocers with barrels of cabbages, onions and potatoes, heaped higher than our heads, and bins full of unshelled peas, watercress and other vegetables we couldn't name, never having eaten them before.

We eventually wound up in a corner favoured by metalsmiths. And that is where we saw the woman in the blood-red dress, picking her way through the stalls, a matching purse dangling from her wrist.

Nothing in that corner should have been of interest to a plump, well-dressed society lady. If we'd been paying attention, we might have wondered what she was doing there and been more careful.

"I want an orange," Agatha said. "A big, juicy orange.'"

"Shh, duck," Spinks said. "You'll get one soon enough. But first, you swoon."

Agatha was the tiniest among us and the best actor, and it was she who would faint dramatically, as if overcome by hunger. She was skinny enough that only those with the hardest of hearts failed to believe her.

Spinks, who still looked wholesome despite his tatty

clothes, was the one who would notice Agatha and shout for help.

And then I would nick the lady's coin purse and run away before she noticed.

As the woman fell into a heated discussion with a glazier, we got into position. Spinks and Agatha rounded the man's stall and I wandered up behind the lady, my hands tucked behind my back, pretending to be looking at his wares.

The woman was showing him a purple glass disc. "I need to grind a set of lenses that can amplify the effects of this one," she said.

"What does this lens do, exactly?" the man asked, holding it up and peering at the sky. "This glass ain't like anything I seen before."

"It's . . . special," the woman said. "It perceives a rare spectrum that—"

That was when Agatha put the back of her wrist against her forehead, rolled her eyes up, and with a sad "Oh!" collapsed at our feet.

"My sister!" Spinks cried, kneeling beside her.

The woman turned and said, "The poor dear! Give her some water." She uncinched the cloth bag on her arm, fetched out a silver flask and held it out to Spinks.

He said, "Oh, thank you, ma'am!" Uncapping it, he tipped it and poured a clear stream on to Agatha's face.

Agatha sputtered dramatically and said, "Is that you, Spinks?"

And that was my cue. Sidling up behind the woman, I slid my right hand into the open mouth of her bag. My fingers came into contact with a latched coin purse, small but heavy, a perfect fit for my fist.

"Oh no, you don't," the woman said, and she cinched the bag tight around my hand, knotting the drawstring.

I yanked but wasn't able to pull free – not while clutching the coin purse. If I'd let go, I might have been able to slide my hand out, but the purse was fat with money and I wanted it.

"Think you're going to rob me, do you?" the woman said, looming over me. I could see now that this was no high-society lady; this was someone who worked hard for a living. It showed in her calloused hands and in the strength of her arms as she lifted me high above the ground by the wrist she'd knotted tight in her purse.

I dangled, my toes kicking at nothing.

"I seem to have caught myself a tiny, filthy rat," the

lady announced. The vendors at the stalls bellowed with laughter.

"Please, ma'am," I gasped. "I'm sorry!"

"Not so sorry that you let go of my purse. Had you done that, foolish boy, I might have turned you loose. But now. . ."

Behind her, Agatha and Spinks melted away into the crowd. They'd go to our hidey-hole off Petticoat Lane, I knew, and wait for me.

The woman lowered me so that my feet touched the ground again. I planted my heels and pulled, and she yanked back so hard that I fell to the pavement, my right arm raised above my head.

"You're coming home with me, rat," she said. "Either on your own bare feet, which would be easier for the both of us, or dragged through the streets. Your choice."

She strutted off through the crowd with me in tow, my knees and shins knocking against every bump and stone on the way

"Let me go, you fat old cow!"

She stopped in her tracks and dangled me in the air once more.

"I'd intended to only bathe you, but it's clear now

that I'll have to scrub your insides as well." She set off again, dropping me once more. This time I landed on my feet and stumbled in her wake.

Our destination was fifteen minutes away: a three-storey inn called the Star-Crossed Arms. By the time we got there, I was crying loudly.

"Stop your sobbing, rat," the woman said. "You want to make a good first impression." And then she pushed open the door.

Inside was a wide hall that split the building in two. To the left was a warm, noisy pub, packed with customers. The smell of meat and potatoes drifting out made my mouth water. To the right were a reception desk and an office. "'Allo, Jenks!" called out a bald man behind the desk. "What you got there?"

"A rat I caught in the market," she said, raising my arm again and looking me over. "Thought I could clean it up and find a use for it."

The bald man made a great show of eyeballing me. "You sure you want to keep this one? Doesn't look too smart."

"Aye, George," said the woman called Jenks. "The church tells us to practice charity, and this sad-looking creature needs all the charity we can spare." And with that, she at last unknotted the purse strings and slipped them off my wrist.

George sighed and grabbed a key ring. "I'll fill a tub," he said.

A little while later, George told me to strip and sit in a vat of hot, soapy water. He gave me a stiff-bristled brush. "See that you scrub away every spot of dirt. Trust me, you don't want to have Jenks do it herself. She's not a gentle one." He shut the door.

I was in a small, windowless, timbered room that had only a fireplace, a trestle table, a looking-glass and a small bookcase full of books. There was no way out, and I was mortally afraid of Jenks, so I did as George had told me and worked at my skin with the brush. There was a cake of sweet-smelling soap. I sat with it at my nose for a minute, sniffing, and then I rubbed it all over until my body and hair both squeaked under my thumb. I hadn't been so clean in years. When I went over to the mirror, I was surprised to see what I looked like.

George brought a pair of soft trousers and a cotton shirt that smelled nice. "Put these on and I'll take you to see herself."

In the office behind the reception, Jenks sat at a desk. She turned as I came in, then pointed to a table in the centre of the room, where steam rose gently from a tin plate full of stew and potatoes. "Fill your belly while I fill your ears," she said. "Just eat and listen."

I threw myself into it like I'd never eaten that well before. Which, come to think of it, may have been the case.

"Now hear me, boy," she told me, "you are young enough that I don't for a moment believe you are a bad sort. You're just a desperate child, driven by hunger to do things that God and society frown upon."

"I'm sorry I tried to rob you, miss," I said. "I won't do it again."

She waved my apology away. "I'm going to make you a proposition. I will feed you, clothe you and educate you for the next six years, if you will agree not to run away or steal from me. Instead, you will work here with me and George, helping us run the inn."

"A job?" I asked. "You're offering me work? But I tried to rob you."

"I'm offering you a *life*," she said. "If you'd rather turn your back on this offer, so be it. I cannot make you choose the path of goodness. But if you'd like a chance to do something meaningful with your life, then you'll find that here."

She stood up then and walked to the exit. "Take some time finishing your dinner, and I'll be back shortly for an answer."

The moment the door closed, I was up off the bench and going through the desk. There were plenty of fine things in its drawers – pens and glass paperweights that I could easily pawn. Sitting square in the centre of the blotter was a fat leather-bound book. Was it valuable? I didn't know, because I couldn't read. I turned the pages and for the first time felt how very stupid I was.

I worried about Agatha and Spinks, but I worried about myself as well. I looked at my clean hands holding the book. They were pink and pristine and looked like new. I'd washed off more than dirt, I realized. I'd washed off my old life.

This Jenks woman would feed me. Give me a place to sleep. Educate me so that the squiggly marks on these pages would actually mean something.

Slowly, I returned the pens and paperweights to where I'd found them, then sat down at the table again.

The stew was delicious. I was thankful that the door was closed, so that no one would see my tears as I used the crusts to mop up every last morsel.

Jenks was as good as her word; better, in fact. Over the years I worked for her, I became healthier, smarter and – something I'd never dreamed possible – happy. She had me learn my letters and within a year I was reading. "You done it, Jack," she said one Christmas, giving me an orange. "You've become respectable."

I turned the orange in my hands, then I asked permission to take a leave of absence. Unfinished business, I told her. I don't know how she knew, but she quietly kissed me on my cheek. "Always be coming home," she said, and sent me off into the cold.

The hidey-hole on Petticoat Lane was through a narrow space under the steps leading up to an abandoned building, but no one had been there in a long while. The wind whistled through the gaps in the stones and it was impossible to get warm. How had I survived here? I wondered. I thought to leave Spinks and Agatha a note, but then I remembered that they wouldn't know what it said. Like the old me, neither of them could read. I believed I'd never see either of them again, but like so much I believed back then, I was wrong.

Unwinding my scarf from around my neck, I placed it on the ground, then nestled the fruit on top. I'd finally brought Agatha her orange.

It was well after midnight when I got home and the downstairs of the inn was dark but for the gas lamp on the front desk.

The night clerk, Ruben, bade me a merry Christmas and let me know Jenks had taken the refuse out back for the raker to cart away. That was my job, but I hadn't been there, so she had taken it upon herself.

I grabbed a lantern and rushed out back, apologies ready.

It was dark behind the inn and I nearly tripped over our sledge. The waste barrels were still upon it, and Jenks was nowhere to be seen.

That was when I heard the sounds of fighting. Raising my lantern, I opened its blinders. The light revealed a strange scene.

Jenks was fighting three men. They'd circled her, but they couldn't get in close – she was whirling between them so fast that she blurred. The men were dressed in ill-fitting dark suits and wore bowlers, and each held a flickering sword. Jenks, meantime, had only a ladle and a stewpot lid.

At the light from my lantern, one man turned. Jenks seized the moment to smack the back of his head with the metal lid. He slumped forward.

She caught the point of the second man's sword with the head of the ladle, then twirled it so that the man lost his grip and his weapon spun away into the dark. She struck him with the stewpot lid as well, and then turned to the third man. "Are you going to attack me or no?" she said.

The man, seeing he faced her alone, backed warily away, then turned and fled.

"Perfect timing," Jenks said, staring at the two unconscious men on the ground in front of her. "Come on, lad, help me dispose of this rubbish."

We put the unconscious men into two of the empty refuse barrels, and when the raker came by with his wagon to haul away our garbage, we loaded them into the back. "Mind you take this waste far, far away from here," Jenks told the raker, handing him a heavy coin purse.

"You're probably wondering what it was you just

saw here," Jenks said to me as we headed back inside. "Those men came here tonight to torture me."

"Why would they want to hurt you?" I asked, shocked and confused.

"Because of who I am, Jack, and what I've sworn to do. I am something called a Blood Guard."

A few years later, I myself joined the Guard. And a few years after that, I did what no one else could do for Jenks: I killed her.

CHAPTER TWENTY

MY WAY ON THE HIGHWAY

"You *killed* Jenks?" I said.

My voice must have been a little ragged, because Dawkins caught my eye. "You OK there, Ronan?"

Maybe it was because Jenks had been like a mother to Dawkins. Maybe because like my mom, she turned out to have a secret life, one in which she served in an age-old company of guardians. Or maybe it was because Dawkins said Jenks had *died*.

It's not that I thought my mom was invincible – I knew she wasn't an Overseer like Dawkins – but she'd deflected bullets using a sword! She'd leaped forty feet through the air! She'd saved my life.

But that didn't mean she couldn't die.

"It was an act of charity." Dawkins drove in silence for a few moments, the only sound the hum of the engine. "Jenks was an Overseer, as I am now. It is a potentially eternal servitude and a lonely one. Your friends and family all pass away, while you carry on. It lasts until another of the Guard volunteers to take your place. Only then is an Overseer allowed to die. By the time Jenks plucked me off the streets, she'd been alive several hundred years. And she was tired. So I helped her."

"By *killing* her?" I asked.

"Not literally. I simply took her place. Then the clock that had stopped for her began ticking again, and within a decade she was gone."

"That's tragic!" Greta said, her fist clutched tight against her chest.

"That was a hundred and seventy years ago, but not a day goes by that I don't miss the old girl," Dawkins replied. He cleared his throat and tapped the clock on the dashboard. "It won't be all that long before we reach Greta's dad's house, but there are still a few hours. Time enough for you two to get some proper rest."

Greta grabbed the duvet from the back bedroom and stretched out on the other padded bench at the dining table, but I stayed put.

I was tired too – my eyes were gritty with fatigue and my body ached, but I didn't think I'd be able to sleep. It was just me and Dawkins now. I'd only met him yesterday – less than twelve hours ago – but it felt like I'd known him my whole life.

I slid the Verity Glass out of my pocket and held it to my eye. The world took on a purple hue, but that was about all.

"Why is the glass this colour?"

"A complex interaction to do with an element called manganese," he answered.

I turned to him, still holding up the lens – and sucked in my breath.

"It's not *that* exciting," he said. "Though maybe if you're interested in optics or—"

"Your head! You've got a—" Unlike Izzy and Henry, Dawkins seen through the lens was wholly there. His body was shadowy in the dark of the cab, his outline completely filled in. But a tiny bundle of flames on his forehead seemed to flicker, rippling and distorting like the reflection of light on water. "It's a—"

"Oh, *that*," he said. "And here I thought you were interested in chemistry."

"What is it?" I asked, mesmerized by the miniature

tongues of light that curled up and wound around each other.

"A flame sigil."

"A sigil," I repeated. "What's that?"

"It's the Guard's mark," Dawkins said. "It reveals to anyone with the means to see it that I have accepted the commission." He covered his forehead with his hand, but I could still see the flames. "A Guard's purity of purpose burns bright. Though it's invisible to the naked eye, I am marked. Just as your mother is marked."

I flipped down the visor mirror on the passenger side. But when I looked at myself through the lens, all I saw was my usual stupid face. I wasn't special, after all. "Why is the Bend Sinister after me?"

He thought for a moment. "I don't rightly know, Ronan. My first guess was that they wanted to use you as leverage, to get your mother to deliver a Pure to them."

"They have my dad," I protested. "Isn't he leverage enough?"

Dawkins patted my shoulder. "You would think so. The Bend Sinister have bigger plans afoot, and somehow you're key to them." He shook his head. "Regardless,

Verity Glasses are not easy to come by and the Bend have none. Please, let's keep it that way. Should you be taken again, smash it."

"Don't you want it?" I asked. "My mom said I should give it to you."

"Keep it for now," Dawkins said. "You might find it useful at some point."

"But I'm not one of the Guard," I said. "I shouldn't be trusted with—"

"Oh, tosh," Dawkins interrupted. "You're on your way. I can tell. See, becoming a Guard changes a person, granting strength, speed and magical abilities. But those talents won't take root unless the candidate has been prepared somehow."

My mother. She had been training me all my life. That first self-defence class when I was five. The gymnastics, the martial arts, the fencing – even the dance classes, ski instruction, and Ultimate intramurals. Every course she'd enrolled me in, all those times she'd made me take this class or that sport so I'd be more "well-rounded", she'd been moulding me into the perfect candidate for the Blood Guard.

It was so exactly like my mom – she never checked in with me about anything. She just told me what I had to do. And I always gave in and went along with her plans. "No one ever asked me if I wanted to join," I said. It sounded whiny even to me.

Dawkins laughed. "Ask? Nobody gets *asked* to be one of the Guard, old boy."

"So was I . . . born into it?" Had my mom given me more than her black hair and dark eyes? "Is that how it works?"

"You're not *born* into the Guard either," Dawkins said. "That fairytale claptrap about being the special prophesied *one* who will save the world?" He wiggled his fingers in the air as though performing magic. "Doesn't happen."

"So it's a choice I make?" I asked.

"Sort of. You don't just wake up one day and decide, *That's it then, I'm going to fight evil!* And then boom, you're in. It's more about . . . integrity. You undergo a thousand small tests over the course of your life. And every time you do the right thing instead of the wrong thing, you become more *worthy* of the Blood Guard. Until one day you are faced with a final make-or-break choice – one that allows you entry into the order, should you wish to join."

"How will I know when that moment comes?" I

asked, looking through the hole in the back of the motor home. Was it when Ms Hand had told me to sit back and watch while she maimed my friend, and I'd obeyed as I always had when people told me what to do? "Maybe it already happened. Maybe I failed."

"Don't worry, Ronan. You've failed nothing and no one. When the time comes, if you're ready, you become something more. And if you're not ready, you don't. Some people – *most* people – are never ready." He turned and gave me his full smile.

I couldn't help myself; I smiled back.

He eased the motor home into the fast lane. The highway had got wider, adding lanes, until there were six on each side. There were cars all around us now, and they were a comfort, each one a little bubble of normality.

"So how did the Bend Sinister figure out my mother is one of the Guard?" I asked.

"That, my friend, is the mystery." Dawkins' smile disappeared. "Your mother isn't even active in the Blood Guard. She took herself off assignment a year ago. These days, aside from her museum job, she just spends her time being your mum."

I closed my eyes and saw her then, as she'd been since

245

we moved to Stanhope. Relaxed, happier, and usually around. As my dad got more and more swallowed up by his work, it was as if she'd expanded, filling the empty space he used to occupy.

"You're skipping school today," she'd announced one morning last winter. "Dress warmly."

It had been dark outside and bitterly cold, and she'd made us thermoses of hot cider and sandwiches. We'd driven for hours, all the way to Vermont, until the sun was high in the sky, the snow making everything almost too bright to look at.

We hiked up a hill through an orchard until we found the perfect Christmas tree. And then she and I cut it down.

"When did you learn to use an axe?" I asked her while we were wrapping the tree in a canvas tarp and tying it to the top of our car.

"Oh, I don't know," she said. "You just pick up skills in life, Ronan."

It was a lot of fun, that Christmas tree expedition with my mom. We were just cold and tired enough afterward that I could almost forget how much fun we *all* used to have – me, Mom and Dad – when we'd buy our tree in Brooklyn and have to drag it home through the snow-covered city streets, the two of them arguing over how best to carry it, me laughing at them.

"She's good at it," I said to Dawkins now. "She's good at being my mom."

"Oh, I don't doubt that," he said. "She's always been the best at whatever she does. We were sorry to see her take some time off, but she felt she had a duty to you."

And suddenly I knew why. "The fire at our house! Was the Bend Sinister behind it?"

"It was," Dawkins said, looking thoughtfully at me. "Or we think it was anyway. We never found any definitive evidence."

"But why would they burn down our house?" I asked. I vividly remembered standing ankle-deep in snow, watching from across the street as the firemen sifted through the blackened bricks and timber that used to be my home.

He threw up his hands. "We don't know! To kill your mum? To rattle her so profoundly that she'd lead them to other members of the Guard – or even to the Pure she was protecting? Whatever their goal, they didn't achieve it – your mother would never compromise her mission."

I aimed the Verity Glass around, but saw nothing new except the tinge of dawn through the windscreen.

"So what's the plan now?" I asked.

"I wish I knew. I'm making this up as I go. My best option right now is to take Greta home to her father, leave the three of you safely there, and pray Mr Sustermann can help me in—"

"Oh, man," I said, remembering. "The motor home has a phone. We can call Greta's dad."

"Tossed it out the window ages ago, " he said. "But Mr Sustermann will have a phone and I shall use that to summon help. Then my associate Ogabe and I will locate your mother and find this Eye of the Needle device. And destroy it."

"Why is Mount Rushmore important?" I asked, thinking of Ms Hand's questions. "It was in your notebook."

Dawkins laughed. "That's just an anagram of something I came across in my research. Rather than writing it down straightforwardly for any old twit to read, I anagrammed it."

"So it was in disguise," I said.

"It's a place called Mourner's Mouth," Dawkins said. "Which I at last have a notion about thanks to the map we found back there."

I thought again about the notebook. "And those dog drawings?" I asked Dawkins. "What do those mean?"

Dawkins shot me a look. "They mean I like dogs, obviously. Who doesn't?"

I don't remember falling asleep, only waking up, groggy, the sun huge and orange through the windscreen, throwing a warm gold over the hundreds of cars around us. None of the cars was moving. We were stuck in a traffic jam.

I found a jar of instant coffee and microwaved two cups. Dawkins turned off the engine and took a cup in each hand. "Ah, the stuff of bad breath and nervous jitters – how I love it!" He downed one immediately.

"Do I smell coffee?" Greta asked, sitting up. The seat cushion seam had left a line across her face.

"I'll make you a cup. You want one too?" I asked Sammy as he yawned himself awake.

"No, thanks," he said. "I'm *eleven*." He wouldn't meet my eye, just picked up his GameZMaster IV and started stabbing at the buttons as if it were some kind of enemy.

Greta sniffed at her green top. "I need a shower. And my clothes stink."

"Welcome to my world," Dawkins called over his shoulder. "But don't you worry – we are just north of Washington, DC. We should have you at your dad's house in a jiffy, provided these cars get a move on before the world ends."

Sipping her coffee, Greta came forward. "How long has traffic been stopped?" she asked.

"A quarter of an hour or so," Dawkins said. "Why?"

"Long enough for people to get out of their cars?" She pointed.

Twenty car lengths away, coming between the lanes of stopped vehicles, were half a dozen shadowy figures. They carried long blades that flickered with light.

"Everyone out, pronto!" Dawkins said. "Use the hole in back. Our friends might notice a side door opening, but I doubt they know about Greta's renovations to the rear of the vehicle."

We went single file, Dawkins following with the swords he'd borrowed from the Bend Sinister compound.

The bedroom was a disaster. Light streamed in from the holes Izzy had stabbed through the ceiling, and bits of broken motor home were scattered all over the carpet. We looked through the jagged, five-foot-wide hole and down into the next car, where a sleepy-looking businesswoman was doing her make-up in the rear-view mirror.

Dawkins pushed aside the dangling aluminium ladder and waved us forward. "Let's not dawdle, kids."

First, he lowered Sammy on to the tarmac, then Greta. He held me back for an instant, whispering, "I'm relying on you to help me protect these two." I dropped down, then Dawkins landed beside me.

"Everyone, stay low and follow me," Dawkins said. He crouched and started to work his way backwards between the lines of stalled cars. But abruptly he stopped short.

"What's wrong?" I asked.

"I thought they were only in front," he said, pointing, "but they're approaching from both directions."

Coming towards us were another four Bend members. They were still fifteen car lengths away, but they'd spotted us. One, a woman, had blonde hair. Ms Hand.

"Guys," Sammy said, his voice rising. "We are totally surrounded. Should we just give up?"

"Don't worry, Sammy," I said. "It'll be OK."

"For you, maybe," he said, looking me full in the eye.

"But *my* foster parents are totally going to fry me. The Head guy will get rid of me, just like he did the Warners' other foster kid."

"Only if they catch us," Dawkins told him. "A big if!"

"Of *course* they're going to catch us! There are four of us with, like, two little swords. You guys are going to get us all killed!"

"Calm down, Sammy," Greta said. She reached up to squeeze his shoulder, but at her touch he whirled away to the edge of the highway, then sprinted down the shoulder, straight towards Ms Hand's group.

"They kidnapped me!" he yelled as he ran. "They made me go with them!"

We watched, stunned.

"I *liked* him," Greta said. "Why's he betraying us?"

"Has he been lying to us the whole time?" I asked.

Dawkins shook his head. "Sammy's just a scared kid, Ronan. His foster parents – well, they sound rather messed up. I'd be afraid of the Bend Sinister Head too."

"But which way should we go?" Greta asked, a desperate edge to her voice.

Dawkins pointed left, at the central reservation.

Traffic on our side was at a dead stop, but across the reservation, on the other side, cars were rocketing past at seventy miles an hour. "That way," he said. "We go that way."

CHAPTER TWENTY-ONE

A THOUSAND LITTLE TESTS

I looked at Dawkins. Was he crazy? "*This* way?" I asked.

Sammy had already reached Ms Hand and her team. They were calmly working their way through the stalled traffic towards the shoulder, not in any particular hurry. I guess they thought we were trapped.

They were right.

"*Over* the central reservation," Dawkins said, leaning down and making a stirrup of his hands. "*Across* the highway."

"*Over* my dead body," Greta said. "*Not* in your wildest dreams."

"No time to argue, Greta. Give me your foot and over

you go." Dawkins extended his clasped fingers. "You two get off the highway while I stop this bunch here."

"I don't like this!" Greta said, putting her right foot into Dawkins' hands.

He flung her up. With a startled yelp, she arced neatly over the crash barrier and on to the other side.

"Listen, Ronan," Dawkins whispered. "Greta is brave and smart, but that's not enough in this fight. You're not a Blood Guard yet, but that doesn't mean you can't protect her. If something happens to me, *you* have to get her to her father. I'm counting on you."

"Sure, but nothing's going to—" I started to say, but he'd already grabbed my foot and thrown me over.

"So what now?" Greta asked, dragging me against the barrier. Cars shot past from right to left, in loud bursts of noise.

I looked back. Behind us, half a dozen of the Bend Sinister agents were closing in on Dawkins, their swords raised.

Four other agents were focused on us. I watched as, fifty feet to our left, the first of them swung himself easily over the barrier.

"They're coming after us!" I shouted.

"That's why you need to *run*!" Dawkins gestured for

us to go; then he stepped out on to the shoulder and faced the six swordsmen coming at him. "Huzzah!" he cried, swinging his swords and galloping their way.

I took Greta's hand, which was cold and sweaty. A moving van thundered past, and I yelled, "Now!" and pulled her across the two empty innermost lanes.

That was as far as we got before a big pick-up truck almost ran us down. Behind us in the fast lanes, a caravan of motorcycles passed, revving their engines.

And then the next lane was clear and it was time to run again.

I stepped forward and tugged at Greta's hand, but she wouldn't move. She was shaking.

"Greta? Only a few more lanes!" I shouted.

"I – I can't." She wouldn't look at me, just stared straight ahead. "I don't want to end up like Dawkins at the truck stop."

Cars swerved around us where we stood in the road. A convertible. Some squat little economy cars. A lumbering white SUV.

"We can do this," I said, yanking her forward.

We were more than halfway across the highway when Greta shrieked, "Ronan!" and stopped again.

Coming across the lanes we'd already traversed were the four agents of the Bend Sinister. While we watched, the lead Bend agent jogged forward into the empty second lane, raising a big sword over his head. I recognized the welt over his brow: Mr Four. His face was as blank as ever, but he was moving faster than usual – probably thrilled to find us frozen there in the middle of the highway.

When he was six feet away, a dump truck struck him. We heard the *whump*, the shrill of its brakes, and then he and the truck were past.

Greta flinched. "They don't even care if they get hit, Ronan."

"We've got to keep going," I told her, squeezing her hand. "We're almost safe. It won't get any worse."

And then it did.

Above the rumble and shush of the traffic, the bleat and blare of horns, rose another noise – a piercing metallic screech. I looked right and saw a school bus skidding, its brakes locked, its back end sliding around as the bus spun sideways. It was empty except for the driver, I noted with relief, at the same moment I realized it was rolling over.

It fell on to its side and slid roof-first down the

highway, hurtling across three lanes right to where we stood frozen in the road.

"Let's go!" I said, but Greta pulled her hand back so hard that I fell to my knees.

So this was how it would end. The two of us crushed by a rolling school bus in a multi-car pile-up. Safeguard your friend, Dawkins had told me. Protect her. And I'd managed to get her all of forty feet. I threw myself at her again and caught her hand in mine. This time, I wasn't going to let go.

The bus was twenty feet away, and we were the same distance from safety at the edge of the highway. We'd never make it.

The three remaining Bend agents were walking forward across the lanes, their swords drawn, apparently not worried about the bus.

Behind them a spindly tall shaft of metal blazed silver in the morning sunlight: Dawkins had leaned the motor home's aluminium ladder up against the crash barrier. It pivoted like a seesaw as he ran up its length and leaped high into the air.

He sailed clear over the heads of the Bend agents and landed mid-stride. And then he blurred, just like my mom had done.

I heard Greta cough, felt her wrist wrenched from my fingers, and she vanished.

Dawkins.

He'd picked her up in his arms and bounded across the last few lanes. In a blink the two of them reappeared on the grassy embankment, far away and safe.

Dawkins had grabbed Greta and left me behind, in the path of the school bus, with three agents at my back.

Abandoning me because I couldn't take care of my friend.

A thousand little tests, he'd said, and I had failed the first one that came my way. So he'd swooped in and left me on the highway like so much trash. Maybe I wasn't Blood Guard material, but did that mean my life wasn't worth anything?

It was. *I* was.

And then I was running.

One step.

The bus was so close now that I was already in its shadow – the remains of its busted windows briefly glinting as it rolled, the wheels and undercarriage coming around to squash me, the noise of it drowning out everything in the world.

A second step.

Time stretched and slowed. The noises around me dropped an octave, as if everything had been plunged underwater, and the light around me dimmed.

And a leap.

I threw myself forward. My jump carried me the last twenty-five feet, over the shoulder and past Dawkins and Greta, all the way to the top of the embankment, where I *twanged* against the chain-link fence and bounced to the ground.

Then time snapped back to normal – colours brightened and sounds sharpened and I was gasping and watching from safety as the school bus bowled over the space I'd been half a second before.

The three Bend agents who'd been behind me disappeared underneath it.

The bus bounced up in the air and kept rolling.

In its wake, the men lay flat on the pavement like splattered bugs.

That could have been me, I thought. *Should* have been me. Except that I'd managed to get out of the way. How?

Below me, Dawkins caught my eye. "Well done, you."

I looked out over the wreckage lining the highway. The school bus had come to a stop on its roof, and I saw the driver punch out one of the windows and clamber down the side.

The broken bodies of the Bend agents littered the road. They should have been dead, but they were slowly moving, limbs that had been twisted into impossible angles straightening themselves, popping into place.

"They're alive," I said. "They're all still alive."

"If you call theirs a life," Dawkins said, standing and pulling Greta up with him. "They're just empty vessels of flesh, Ronan. Like golems. Or remote-control robots. There are only two ways to stop them for good. One is to burn them so that they can't come back."

As he spoke, I felt someone staring at me: Ms Hand, standing on the far side of the barrier, her arms crossed. Beside her was Sammy. He gripped the fence, something silvery between his wrists: cuffs, I realized. Ms Hand had handcuffed him.

"She's got Sammy," I said.

"That's unfortunate," Dawkins said. "I do wish he hadn't run off like that."

Ms Hand's gaze chilled me until I was shivering. Dawkins helped me to my feet and said, "The other way to stop them? Break their Hand."

I looked at Greta, who was practically comatose, and

at bloodied and bruised Dawkins. I was angry at him for abandoning me on the highway, but mostly I was angry at myself. I'd been tested, and I had failed, again and again. We'd been running all night from this woman and her vacant-eyed henchmen, and they were still after us. They were never going to give up. Maybe it was time to stop running.

"Break their Hand?" I repeated. "Then that's what we have to do."

"All in good time," Dawkins promised. "All in good time."

CHAPTER TWENTY-TWO

GRETA, PURE
AND SIMPLE

Compared to what we'd just come through, scaling the fence at the crest of the embankment was a cinch. We ended up on a street of small businesses — gas station, convenience store and, at the corner, a fast-food restaurant where a silvery sports car sat idling in the drive-through.

"That'll do," Dawkins announced and broke into a run.

The young man behind the wheel looked half asleep, though he snapped awake when Dawkins opened the car door, grabbed him by the lapels of his black leather jacket and lifted him from the driver's seat. He set the startled man on his feet, spun him around and pushed him away.

"What are you doing?" the man cried. "Help!"

"I am terribly sorry," Dawkins said. "Greta, take the back seat. Ronan, shotgun." We got in.

"You're not taking anything, buddy," the man said, raising his fists like a boxer.

At that moment, the drive-through window slid open and an arm reached out with a bag and a coffee. Dawkins took the bag and threw it over the man's head, crying, "Catch!"

Startled, the man reached up.

That gave Dawkins enough time to leap into the driver's seat and peel out of the forecourt. He looped the car through a series of turns until we'd reached a wide multi-lane street. "Wisconsin Avenue," he announced. "It stretches all the way from Maryland, where we are now, into Georgetown, where we will find Mr Sustermann's house."

"I can't believe you just stole that man's car!" I protested.

"Why are you still surprised when I do things like this, Ronan?" Dawkins replied. "Honestly, I'd think you would have come to expect it from me by now."

A little more than an hour later, Dawkins turned down a tree-lined street of pretty brownstone houses. They reminded me of home – Brooklyn, not Stanhope.

"We're here." They were the first words any of us

had said in ages. Dawkins drove a full circle around the block before pulling to the kerb and shutting off the engine. "Just want to be absolutely sure that there are no ugly guests going to drop in on us. There is no reason whatsoever to believe the Bend Sinister have identified Greta . . . but one can never be too safe."

"Greta?" I said, shaking her. "Greta, you're home."

Her head jerked up and she was instantly awake. "Home?"

"Your father's place." Dawkins gestured at a brick building with white trim.

Greta sat up straight, wiped her eyes and pulled at the tangled mess of her hair. "I need a scrunchie."

"Why don't you go and have a little father-daughter reunion, and once that's over, Ronan and I will come in and have a sit-down. I'll explain what happened, maybe ask for his assistance."

She opened the back door of the car. "All right, I'm going. Ronan, you're OK?"

"I'm fine," I said. "Go and see your dad."

We watched as she vanished behind the bushes near the front door.

"You left me to *die*," I said, staring straight ahead. "You grabbed Greta."

"I couldn't very well carry both of you," Dawkins said. "And I figured you had the better chance of survival."

"The better chance? Are you telling me you took a minute to figure out the odds?"

Dawkins sighed. "No, I didn't calculate any odds. I grabbed Greta," he said slowly, "because she is a Pure."

"What?" I turned to him. He looked very serious, and very old. "A Pure? You're saying Greta is one of those thirty-six special people?"

"I'm saying it's a good thing you never looked through that Verity Glass at *her*. It would have been the opposite of those two grey-haired goons with the motor home. The blaze of Greta's soul would have momentarily blinded you."

"Greta Sustermann is a Pure," I repeated.

"Yes, Ronan. Your mother, Bree, was one of her guardians back in Brooklyn, but after that house fire, she took a break from the Guard."

I shook my head, confused. "But Greta's no saint. She's just – she's kind of full of herself and mouthy, to be honest."

"The Pure aren't *saints*, Ronan. Not goody-goodies. They're just deeply, unavoidably *good* people. They make everyone better – just by existing."

And all at once I knew it was true.

I'd done more and been braver in the past sixteen hours than at any time in my life until now. Was that because Greta had been beside me? She cared so much about doing the right thing that maybe it had rubbed off on me a tiny bit. I searched my feelings and I knew that I didn't want her to think less of me. Instead, some part of me wanted the opposite – to be worthy of her good opinion. Was that what a Pure did for everyone?

"I don't understand. If there are supposed to be Guards for Greta, why weren't they with her on the train?"

"That's why I was there," Dawkins said, slapping his chest. "When Greta goes back and forth between her parents, I – or Ogabe, or another Overseer – tag along, make sure the hand-over from the two Guards in Brooklyn goes smoothly."

"You weren't there because of me?" I said.

"That's why I had your mother put you on that particular train. It was a two-birds-with-one-stone sort of thing. Had I known there were going to be so many Bend agents after you, I would have called for reinforcements." He exhaled sharply. "It turned into such a mess. She was never supposed to cross paths with you."

"And that's why you grabbed Greta instead of me."

"Of course. I would have felt terrible if that bus had taken you out, Ronan, but I had no choice in the matter: *I had to save Greta*. Because she's not supposed to die."

"Is that why the Bend Sinister are chasing us? Because she's a Pure?"

"Afraid not. If they had any idea of what Greta is, your Ms Hand would never have let her escape." He poked me in the shoulder. "No, they're pursuing us because of you. But I don't yet know why."

"Two Guards in Brooklyn, you said. Two here in Washington, DC." Something became clear to me. "And you knew where Greta's father lives. Is Greta's father one of the Guards?"

Dawkins ran his fingers through his hair and said, "Yes, her father is one of the Blood Guard. We recruited him shortly after Greta was born. He was already a lawyer, so he was a prime candidate. That's also why her father has always been so – adamant, shall we say? – about making sure she knows how to take care of herself. It's not just that he's with the FBI, as Greta keeps prattling on about. He believes in self-reliance. Like your mum."

A banging on the window startled us.

It was Greta, back from her dad's house, and seeing the horrified expression on her face, we got out of the car in a hurry.

"What is it?" Dawkins said, taking her by the shoulders. "Greta, what's wrong?"

"My dad," she said in a low voice. "He's not there! The – the place is trashed, and there's blood in the hallway, and – and – and—"

"Breathe, Greta," Dawkins said.

She took a deep, shaky lungful of air. "And in his downstairs office, there's a body."

CHAPTER TWENTY-THREE

OGABE LOSES HIS HEAD

Greta carefully led us through the wreckage of her father's living room. There wasn't a book still on a shelf, a picture still on a hook. Everything had been thrown to the floor.

"What were they looking for?" I asked.

"Anything that could lead them to more of the Guard," Dawkins said. "Or a Pure."

"I don't understand," Greta said. "Why would they go after my dad?" She took us down a short staircase into her father's office. There was an enormous desk in the middle of the room, covered with papers and piles of things. Its drawers had been pulled out and the contents cast everywhere.

"Where's this body you mentioned?" Dawkins asked.

"Over there, where the chair goes," she said, her voice wavering. "He's missing his head, but he's pretty obviously not my dad."

"They took his *head*?" Dawkins said.

"Maybe I'll just wait over here," I said, standing by the door.

"Ogabe!" Dawkins cried, crouching down behind the desk. "What have they done to you!"

He reappeared a moment later, helping an enormous headless body to stand up. Ogabe was a dark-skinned man, more than six feet tall even without his head. He was dressed in a bloodstained pin-striped blue suit, a starched white dress shirt and a classy tie. But where his head should have been on his neck, there was just a smooth patch of dark brown puckered skin. I don't know what severed necks usually looked like – bloody muscle and bone? – but this definitely wasn't that. Ogabe straightened the cuffs of his jacket and smoothed down his lapels.

"Greta, Ronan, meet Ogabe. I'm sure he'd say something like, 'A pleasure to meet you,' if only he had a mouth to talk with and ears to hear with."

Dawkins placed Ogabe's hands on his face, and the

fingers carefully felt Dawkins' features, then combed through his long greasy hair. When he had finished, Ogabe's body embraced Dawkins in a massive hug, lifting him into the air.

Dawkins patted Ogabe's back and said, "There, there, big fellow!"

Once he was set back down, Dawkins righted the desk chair and guided the man to it.

"How can he even move?" Greta asked. "He doesn't have a *head*."

"Your powers of observation are impressively keen," Dawkins said.

I didn't say anything, too transfixed by the sight of the man, now sitting comfortably at the desk, feeling around with his hands on the polished wood.

"He's an Overseer, like me," Dawkins explained. "So he can't be killed – not even when you cut off his head and run away with it. Which is why the Bend Sinister did exactly that, to stop him from revealing their actions. They thought they'd silenced him, but they were wrong."

"You mean he can still talk?" Greta said, her voice cracking.

"He has no mouth, Greta – how could he talk?" Dawkins rested his hand on Ogabe's shoulder. "But wherever it is, Ogabe's head can still communicate with his body. No matter how great the distance separating them, the two remain linked. Something we can very much take advantage of."

"Shouldn't we get him to a hospital?" Greta asked, clutching my hand so hard it hurt. "Isn't he in danger of *dying* or something?"

Dawkins waved her off. "A hospital can do nothing for him. The only thing that can make things right is to reunite his head with his body. Might require a bit of duct tape or epoxy or something," he said thoughtfully. "But we can burn that bridge when we come to it."

Greta gazed around the wreckage of the room, her brow furrowed. "But I don't get it – why is a Blood Guard Overseer here, and my dad missing?"

"A very good question," Dawkins said, looking her in the eye. "The answer is that your dad, like Ronan's mother, is a member of the Blood Guard. Sorry you had to find out this way."

"You are *crazy*," Greta said, crossing her arms. "According to you, *everyone* is a member of this stupid Blood Guard thing."

"Not everyone. Just Ronan's mum and your dad. And me, of course."

"I don't believe you. If my dad were part of something like that, I'm the one person in the world he would tell."

"Doubtless that's true, Greta," Dawkins said, "but the proof is all around us. We're conversing over a body without a head — a body that is fully functioning and, from the looks of it, impatient." Ogabe was drumming his fingers on the desktop. "And you saw me killed back there at that truck stop, only to come back and rescue the two of you."

"We were doing a fine job of rescuing ourselves," I said.

"Yes, yes, Ronan — you were a master with that chair. But, Greta, there is no other explanation: the Blood Guard is real, and your father, a good man, is one of us."

"I'll believe it when I hear it from my dad."

As they talked, I'd leaned in closer towards the body. "Why is his neck smooth like that?" I asked. The skin was faintly shiny, like a healed burn.

"When an Overseer loses a limb, the wound seals over. It's bloody at first, and painful like you would not believe, but then the enchantment takes over and the wound closes." Dawkins found a pencil in the papers on the desk.

He placed the pencil in the man's hand, then positioned it over a sheet of paper.

The hand scribbled for a moment, and Dawkins squinted down at what it was writing.

"What's he say?" I asked.

"It's hard to read," Dawkins said, scowling. "It's a good thing you can't hear me, friend, because your penmanship is *terrible*."

I came around and looked at the paper. "I think it says, 'You're late, as usual.'"

"That sounds like Ogabe." Dawkins began rooting through the piles on the desk. "We need something he can type with. But they took your father's computer." There was a monitor, but the cable from its back hooked up to nothing.

"My old laptop is upstairs in my toy box," Greta said. "I'll get it." She dashed out and returned a few minutes later with a fat pink child's laptop. She'd already turned it on, so Dawkins set it on the desk and positioned Ogabe's hands. The fingers found the space bar and carefully poised themselves over the keys.

Then he daintily touch-typed. *Not really sure how we're going to communicate, since I don't have any ears, but I'll tell you what I know.*

"It's like his body is on remote control," I said.

"It's exactly like that. Only we've lost the remote." Dawkins took Ogabe's hand, flipped it over, and using a pencil, slowly wrote out letters in his open palm. As he did, he spoke the words aloud. "What happened?"

Gaspar was worried about his daughter, Ogabe typed.

"Gaspar is my dad," Greta whispered, her voice quavering.

Dawkins quickly wrote something else in Ogabe's palm.

After a moment, the typing resumed. *Here?*

"I'm letting him know we brought you here," Dawkins said. "You and Ronan." He wrote on Ogabe's hand for a while, probably reminding him not to discuss Greta's true nature while she was in the room. After that, the man put his hands back on the keyboard and began typing fast, piling up sentence after sentence.

The Bend must have been watching this place. The doorbell rang and when Gaspar answered, it was flung open and a team of Bend Sinister agents burst in.

Dawkins wrote something more on Ogabe's hand with the pencil.

In response, Ogabe's fingers typed out, *They had the element of surprise. We fought them but there were too many, and* we were unarmed. *They knocked Gaspar unconscious, and then chased me into his office and piled on me. Took five of them to hold me down.* He paused for a moment. *Their Hand almost seemed to enjoy being the one to lop off my—* He stopped abruptly and his hands closed into fists.

"I'm sorry, friend," Dawkins said, writing on Ogabe's palm.

I recovered from the shock a while ago and have been quietly observing my surroundings ever since. I can still see and hear and, if they get close enough, bite – not that they've been that foolish. Mostly they've kept my head in a pillowcase. But it doesn't matter. I think I know where they've taken me. Is Bree with you?

Dawkins shook his head and wrote.

That's too bad.

Dawkins wrote and said, "So where are you? We're all ears here."

Could you be any more insensitive? I'm trying to help you and you make little jokes.

"That wasn't – oh, never mind." Dawkins wrote something more. "Go on."

We're underground. We arrived by boat – I could smell the river and hear the water slapping the hull, and when they finally took my head out of the bag, I caught a glimpse of a small dock at the entrance of a cave. We're at Mourner's Mouth, I'm certain of it. They threw me on to a bed in a tiny office, one of several they've turned into jail cells.

Dawkins looked up at us. "We'd intercepted a Bend Sinister communication that mentioned a place with that name," he said, "but we were never able to find out what it meant. Only that Mourner's Mouth was a key location for the Bend Sinister."

Mourner's Mouth is a cave system on the Potomac River that later became home to the East Potomac Park Substation, a small hydroelectric power plant that was closed back in the 1970s. You'll find all of our research – including a map of the place – in a file Gaspar has on his computer.

"They took his computer," Dawkins said as he wrote. "But I believe I have a map." He reached into his jacket and drew out the blueprint he'd taken from the Bend Sinister safe house. He unfolded it on the desk, ran his finger along one edge, and then went back to writing on Ogabe's hand. "It's a two-storey underground complex. Here is the row of offices where they're probably holding you, and here is the dock entrance. This must be the place."

Whatever the Bend Sinister is doing, it requires a lot of energy. More than they can pull off a city's power grid. They reopened an old substation, modernized its equipment and got it up and running again. Gaspar figured out that much, but he never learned why *they need so much power.*

"We have that part figured out," Dawkins wrote.

I don't know why they took Gaspar, but it can't be good. One of them mentioned "test subjects" during the drive to Mourner's Mouth.

"They'd better not do anything to my dad," Greta said, her voice low.

"We'll find him," I said. I wanted to reassure her, but I wasn't really sure how to do that, so I just gave her an awkward one-armed shoulder hug. "We're going to get him – and my parents – back, and we'll stop these Bend Sinister people. That's what friends do, help each other, right?" I'd never in a million years have called Greta a friend before we met on the train yesterday, but I felt different about her now.

She snorted. "You don't sound so sure."

"I haven't had all that many friends," I said. "I'm kind of new at this."

Dawkins had been slowly writing a series of questions to Ogabe, and after each one, the man's fingers danced across the keyboard.

There were six who came here to Gaspar's; a Hand and a team of five agents. But I'd be surprised if they were the only team at Mourner's Mouth.

"How do we surprise them?"

Gaspar discovered another way in. The substation is connected to the DC storm drains. That way, when the hydroelectric plant overflows, the excess water floods into the storm drains and back to the river. All we have to do is work backwards, following the storm drains into the substation.

Dawkins wrote a few words in Ogabe's palm, and the body stood up from the chair.

Dawkins looked at me and Greta. "I am conflicted. It's far too dangerous to leave you two here unattended. And yet it's far too dangerous to take you with us."

"No way am I going to wait around while you and a headless body try to rescue my dad," Greta said. "Talk about hopeless teams!"

"Oh, Ogabe isn't going to be doing any rescuing," Dawkins said. "He can't even see where he's going. I'll be leaving him in that car we borrowed."

"Dawkins," Greta said, "you're going to need help. We're coming with you."

"You two have no training," Dawkins said. "Yes, yes," he added, as I began to object, "you've taken classes in hand-to-hand combat and fencing and who knows what else, but we're facing a dozen of the Bend Sinister, all of them intent on killing you."

The sound of typing made us all turn back to Ogabe. He was hunched over the laptop again, furiously pecking at the keys.

STOP ARGUING, JACK.

That's what you always do, just sit around talking while everyone waits. Lives are at stake. The clock is ticking. The risks are too high to chance losing.

And don't even THINK about leaving me in the car.

"He really knows you well, doesn't he?" I said to Dawkins, closing the laptop and putting it in Ogabe's hands. "But he's right. Like it or not, we're all in this together."

CHAPTER TWENTY-FOUR

DOWN A GIANT'S THROAT

"So *this* is how we get in?" Greta asked.

"Since none of you will listen and stay in the car," Dawkins grumbled, "I suppose so."

It was a little past nine in the morning, and we were standing on the grass of a deserted park, in the shadow of an enormous arm, part of an eerie metal sculpture of a giant working his way out of the ground at the very tip of East Potomac Park.

The giant's right arm stretched twenty feet up, the shoulder and bicep flexing, its fingers clawing at the air. Thirty feet away, the left hand had only just broken through the soil, the wrist still underground. The toes of the giant's right foot were visible some distance away, and the bent left knee arced high enough off the ground that I could walk under it if I ducked my head. The whole thing was made of a dusky silver metal that was cold to the touch.

The giant's face looked blindly up at the blank sky, his mouth open wide. Was he angry? Suffering? Sad to be waking up in a world that no longer believed in him?

"Mourner's Mouth makes sense," I said. "He does look sad."

"It *is* a bit spooky," Dawkins admitted.

"Spookier than driving around with a headless man in the passenger seat of the car?" I asked.

Dawkins glanced at Ogabe and said, "Only that one woman noticed – and who's going to listen to her? Headless man in a sports car? That's crazy talk!"

"This sculpture is actually called *The Awakening*," Greta said. "My dad took me here last winter. He said he wanted to show me something cool. But I guess he was just casing the site."

"There's no reason he couldn't have been doing both," I said.

"Stop lollygagging, you two," Dawkins called. He led Ogabe straight to the giant's bearded face. Its silver tongue curved back into shadow, past enormous teeth. I felt cold air wafting up out of the mouth. On the drive over, Ogabe had explained that there was a shaft directly under the giant's mouth that connected to the storm drains.

"Everyone got their torches?" Dawkins asked, holding his aloft. We nodded, and he placed Ogabe's hands on the giant's lower lip. "This had better work."

Ogabe bellied head first into the giant's mouth. After a moment of kicking his legs in the air and Dawkins pushing him by his feet, he slid into the dark and disappeared.

Dawkins leaned forward into the mouth, then backed out in a hurry.

The giant seemed to cough up a round metal disc. It flew out of the mouth and rolled on the ground like some sort of enormous button.

"It appears Ogabe got the grill off the manhole," Dawkins said, swinging his legs into the mouth. "Will be a bit of a drop, but I'll be there to catch you two." He let go and plunged out of sight.

"You next," I said to Greta.

She grabbed the giant's nose for balance and slid her sneakers into its mouth. "This is . . . kind of creepy," she said, scooting backwards. "Though plenty of stuff in the past day has been loads creepier." When just her hands and head were visible around the curve of the giant's tongue, she said, "Thanks, Ronan."

"For what?" I asked.

"I don't know. For everything? For helping me look for my dad. For putting up with me when I'm less than awesome. For being, whatever – a friend."

And then she let go, slipping away before I could reply. I wanted to tell her that *she* was the one who deserved thanks, not me. That I wasn't like her. Whenever I did something good, it was by accident, or because someone had told me what to do. But Greta tried to do the right thing just because it was the right thing.

I took one last look around at the empty park, then climbed into the giant's mouth. The wide metal tongue was cold against my belly, and it stank like stale, grimy water. I turned and let my feet dangle.

"We're not getting any younger," Dawkins called from below.

I let go and fell about ten feet – right into Dawkins' arms.

"Ogabe and Greta have already gone down," he said,

setting me on my feet. We were in a tiny concrete chamber barely large enough for the two of us. At our feet was a round concrete shaft, metal rungs like enormous staples leading down into the gloom. "Greta shouldn't be here at all, but there was no way to stop her from looking for her father. So I'm relying on you to stay back and protect her."

"You can count on me," I told him.

"I know that," Dawkins said, placing his feet on the rungs. "I just wanted to make sure that *you* know it too."

We went down.

Greta and Ogabe were waiting at the foot of the ladder, their torches on. We were in an enormous concrete tube, maybe twelve feet high. The storm drain.

"Which way?" Greta asked.

I cast my light over the map Ogabe had had us print out. "Looks like we hike north," I said. The two storm drains and the substation weren't connected on the map, but Ogabe assured us there was a link between them.

Dawkins led. Twelve feet of rope connected him and Ogabe. Behind them was Greta, and I brought up the rear.

Eventually the tunnel ended at a metal grill. It stretched from wall to wall and floor to ceiling, like the bars of a jail cell. Stringy bits of moss drooped from the crossbars. "This is what Ogabe told us about," Dawkins said. "We should now be level with the top storey of the substation."

Ogabe stood in front of the grill as though he were looking it over – though of course, he couldn't see a thing without his head. He reached up and pulled at the bars, but they didn't budge.

Dawkins played his light across it. "Typically there's a gate somewhere – there!" Along the right-hand wall, his beam caught a rusty padlock.

Greta examined it. "I can't pick something this old without the right equipment."

Dawkins smiled and produced a leather pouch. "Miss Sustermann," he said, "may I present to you your father's lock-pick set."

Greta's smile in return was huge, and her voice wavered as she said, "I've missed these!" She ran her thumbs over the worn leather of the pouch, then untied the laces and unrolled it. Inside were four pockets filled with hooked metal blades. "These are as good as a set of keys."

She got to work. At first I'd found it strange that she and her dad shared this hobby, but I couldn't help feeling a little jealous. My dad and I never did anything together these days. At least she and her dad bonded over lock-picking.

With a click, the padlock fell open.

"I'm sure Gaspar would be proud," Dawkins said, smiling. "All right, we are now entering the substation. The plan: I park you two somewhere – anywhere safe – while I go in search of Ogabe's head. I reattach it, and then he and I find your dad, Greta, and the three of us destroy this Eye of the Needle thing."

"No," Greta said. "You need help – that's what Ogabe said. So we're going to help."

"I've let you come this far," Dawkins said, "because it was too dangerous to leave you at your dad's house or up in that empty stolen car. But I will *not* have you in harm's way."

"Fine, we'll stay out of harm's way, but we're still coming with you," Greta said. "Right, Ronan?"

I thought about how she'd thanked me earlier, and then about how our parents were somewhere up ahead. "Greta's right. You need all the help you can get," I said. "We can come with you and still be safe, I promise."

Dawkins threw up his hands. "I don't know why I waste my breath with you two." He swung open the gate and we all passed through.

We turned down one tunnel after another until we heard a deep thrumming up ahead. Dawkins turn off his torch and we followed suit.

"What is that?" Greta asked.

"Generators," Dawkins whispered.

The tunnel ended in the corner of a large, warehouse-like room. The floor was a checquerboard of squares made of clear-glass brick and steel planking. And filling the room were eight enormous devices, each about as big as a garbage truck. They were the source of the humming.

"Turbines," Dawkins whispered, pointing. "River water gets pushed up those massive fat tubes there" – giant pipes rose from the floor and curved around the central engine housing for each of the turbines – "and the water pressure turns the blades in those generators, creating electricity. It's supposed to be decommissioned, but as you can see, the Bend Sinister has it up and running again."

Control panels the size of refrigerators were set in a

row down a central aisle, one at the foot of each turbine. Strung from the high ceiling were banks of floodlights, but they weren't turned on. What light there was in the room rose up from below, through the squares of glass.

"The Bend Sinister must need a lot of power for. . ."

"The Eye of the Needle?" I asked, but Dawkins didn't answer.

We moved in single file out of the tunnel – Dawkins, Ogabe, Greta and then me – and crouched down between the humming turbines. Along the way, Dawkins paused to peek down through the glass squares in the floor. "It appears that operations are visible through the floor of this room," he said. They were like skylights into the rooms below. The first bunch we looked through revealed an empty room packed with plastic-shrouded desks and dark computers. On the far wall was a pair of white doors, the only way in or out other than the tunnel we came through.

"Clearly we can get downstairs through those," Dawkins said, pointing. "But before we do, let's make a systematic search for our friends via these glass-brick windows – taking pains not to be visible to anyone who might be below. Greta, you take the right side of the room; Ronan, the left; we'll park Ogabe beside the exit;

and I'll check out the middle."

I had checked only ten glass squares – some empty rooms, another four that seemed to follow a hallway – when I looked down and saw something round lying on a bed: a dark-skinned head. It looked at me and blinked, then broke into a huge smile.

"Hey!" I whispered. "I see Ogabe!"

"Never mind that," Greta hissed. "Something very weird is going on over here!" She was on her knees against the right wall, just out of reach of the light from the room below.

Dawkins and I crouched down next to her and looked down upon a strange scene.

The chamber below was a bizarre cross between an operating room and a computer lab. There were banks of monitors and keyboards along one wall, and, in the middle, five people gathered around a stainless-steel operating table. One of them was speaking, a grey-haired man in a lab coat and surgical mask. He was waving one hand in the air as, with the other, he guided a big metal ring to the head of the table. It was attached to a pivoting metal arm like a dentist's X-ray machine and was about the size of a hula hoop, but made out of segmented chrome parts and bristling with wires and cables.

Whatever they were doing, I didn't like the look of it. "We should get back," I said. "Before someone sees us."

"Shh," Dawkins said, quietening us. We could hear the faintest of murmurs, like people talking in a distant room. "Sounds like there may be a way to hear what they're saying."

Dawkins withdrew a screwdriver from his pocket. Then he went to a row of ventilation grills along the base of the wall and removed one. Immediately the murmur became slightly clearer. "Right," he said, wiggling into the shaft behind the grill. A few minutes later, he backed out, grey with dust, holding a pair of filters. "Had to remove a few obstructions," he said.

"Shh! They can hear you," Greta whispered.

Everyone in the room had stopped what they were doing. They were gazing up towards the glass panels.

We scooted back until we were out of sight, fully hidden from below by darkness. But we could still see them, frozen and staring upward.

At last, from the vent, we heard the faint echo of a man's voice. "It's nothing. This old substation makes all sorts of noises – it's like a house settling on its foundations."

Another voice, a woman's, said, "It sounded like people talking."

"You worry too much," said the man in the surgical mask. "As I was saying, the Eye of the Needle is nearly ready. Please switch the lights off, Donald." The lights in the room below dimmed for a moment, and the metal hoop filled with a net of brilliant red light.

The crisscrossed grid of beams was so bright that it took our eyes a moment to adjust. "It's beautiful," one man exclaimed, and everyone in the group seemed to agree.

We edged closer again as the man in the surgical mask positioned the hoop. "As you can see, the table is on rails, allowing us to easily pass our subjects through the Needle's Eye. The soul is combed out and trapped here, in the Conceptacle." He tapped his finger against a silvered glass bottle and screwed it into place on the side of the hoop. "This is a double-walled silvered flask, which has undergone a complicated enchantment that effectively traps the soul for as long as we wish to keep it."

"And what happens to the . . . subject?" the woman asked.

The man in the mask paused for a moment. "I

suppose the subject *could* be kept alive in a vegetative state, hooked up to breathing machines and the like, though I can't imagine why anyone would bother." And then he laughed like he'd said something funny.

I was so tense with anger that I felt like I could throw up. After the past eighteen hours, I'd got used to the fear. But anger? That fed something new: a determination to stop these people. I'd felt the first inklings of it on the side of the highway while looking at Ms Hand. But now it was overwhelming. Somebody had to stop the Bend Sinister, and wasn't that what my mom had secretly raised me to do?

Greta's breathing quickened. "He said *subject*," she whispered. "Ogabe said something about that. Are they going to use my dad as a test subject?"

"Before we comb the soul from our first Pure," the man continued, "we have to make a few test runs – to calibrate the Eye, so we can be sure the Conceptacle is properly hosting the subject's essence." The man gestured and the net of light in the hoop disappeared. "Donald?" he said. "Bring out the boy."

A moment later, a familiar voice said, "Dr Warner – I mean, Dad? What's going on?" And then a frizzy head of dark hair entered the room, escorted by a brawny guy in a suit. "Am I forgiven?"

"Absolutely, Samuel," Dr Warner said. "We know you were an innocent pawn in the hands of those people."

Even from up above, through the glass of the floor, I could see Sammy's shoulders relax. "That's what I told everyone, but no one listened."

"It's OK, son," Dr Warner said. "We brought you here to ask for your help. We're testing a new scanner and need someone to examine."

"A scanner," Sammy said, and I could see him tense up as he looked around. Then he nodded. "Sure. OK. What do you need me to do?"

"Just lie down on the trolley. We'll guide it through this metal hoop here. You might feel a slight pull, a tugging inside you. But ignore it. It won't last long."

"Do as your father tells you," said a petite lady with short blonde hair who was wearing a lab coat.

"OK, Mom." Sammy climbed up on to the trolley. "No problem."

I pressed my hands to the glass, wanting to shout to Sammy, to warn him, but I couldn't seem to draw a breath or get a word out. *They can't do this.* But it was too late: Sammy was already on the table, the straps tightened around his wrists, chest and ankles.

Greta opened and closed her mouth, unable to say anything, and turned to Dawkins, but he was already up and running, the screwdriver clenched in his fist.

CHAPTER TWENTY-FIVE

MAN ON FIRE

"Make noise!" Dawkins yelled. "Get their attention! Slow them down!"

Greta pounded her fists on the glass so that everyone looked up. "Sammy!" she cried. "Get out of there!"

"Greta?" Sammy said, smiling and squinting past the lights. "What are you doing up there?"

"Donald," Dr Warner said calmly, "send someone to take care of this disturbance." He gently pressed Sammy back against the trolley. "Never mind them, son."

"Don't trust him!" I yelled. "He's lying to you!"

"Ronan!" Dawkins shouted. "I need your assistance."

He fell to his knees beside one of the enormous generators and wedged the blade of the screwdriver under the steel planking on the floor. Beneath the steel was a channel filled by a fat braided cable covered in black plastic.

"What's that?" I said as I reached him.

"Conduit," he said breathlessly. "All the power from those generators there goes through these cables here to the station below us."

"They're going to kill you, Sammy!" Greta shouted, banging on the glass.

"Here's what's going to happen," Dawkins told me. "I am going to stab this screwdriver into that cable. That will create a short in the system and cause all the power to shut down."

"But you'll . . . get electrocuted," I said. "You'll die."

"That's usually what electrocuted means, yes," he said. "But die? Me? Never!" He slipped out of his leather jacket. "Nonetheless, once the power is off, I *am* going to need you to pound on my chest with your fist to bring me back."

"Pound your chest, got it."

"You will have to hit me very *hard*. You're basically kick-starting my heart. Otherwise, it will just take its sweet time, the lazy thing, and I need to be up faster than that."

Greta shouted, "Sammy's got one of his arms free!"

"Good to hear," Dawkins called. "Greta, go and join Ogabe by the door."

He whispered a few words and the blade of the screwdriver grew incandescent. "Remember: don't touch me until the power has cut off. If you touch me before then, I may still be conducting electricity. Oh, and I almost forgot: please put me out if I catch fire." He handed his leather jacket to me. "Use this to beat the flames."

Then he clutched the screwdriver with both hands, raised it over his head and slammed it into the cable.

There was a blinding burst of dazzling light, followed by a sudden silence as everything shut down. The room went completely dark. After a moment, I saw something in front of me flickering orange.

I blinked and turned on my torch.

The flicker was Dawkins. The electrical short had blasted him backwards, away from the cable. In the torch's beam, I could see tendrils of smoke rising gently from his body. His jaw was slack, his eyes open and empty.

And his T-shirt was on fire.

I froze for a second, thrown back to that nightmare

moment in Brooklyn when I'd woken up to flames crackling around the edges of my bedroom door.

And then I snapped out of it. This was my *friend* on fire – a friend who was depending on *me* to save *him* for a change.

I smacked the leather jacket on him, using it to douse the flames.

And then I did as I'd been told: I pounded my fist against his sternum. Once, twice, three times.

Nothing happened.

"Come *on*," I grunted. I sat astride him on the floor, clasped my fists together and brought them down as hard as I could.

He inhaled loudly, then coughed, arching his back.

I couldn't help myself: I laughed. He was alive! He couldn't be killed, but still I'd been worried – that I'd let him down; that I'd let him die.

He said something unintelligible, flexed his fingers and hands, then said, "Why . . . are you . . . *sitting* . . . on me?"

Laughing again, I pulled him up, threw his arm over my shoulder, and half dragged him to where Greta and Ogabe stood beside the doors, their backs against the wall, holding hands. There was the sound of a chain rattling from the other side of the doors.

"I think someone's coming," Greta said.

"The door will hide us," Dawkins whispered, "but we will have to move quietly."

Across the room, I saw the torch I'd forgotten on the floor. I started for it, but Dawkins held me back. "It will lead them that way."

Greta let go of Ogabe's hand and hugged Dawkins. "You saved Sammy!"

"Yes, yes," Dawkins whispered. "Now shut up."

The doors were pushed open, and four men wielding powerful torches ran into the room. Each was perfectly groomed and dressed in the dark business suits that seemed to be the Bend Sinister uniform. In the light of their beams I could see that three of them held swords, while the fourth carried a Tesla rifle. Without speaking, they went straight towards the beam from my torch.

Dawkins caught the edge of the door before it closed, and the four of us quietly slipped through, Greta leading Ogabe by the hand. On the floor in front of the door was an open padlock and chain that Dawkins ran through the door handles. He snapped the padlock shut. "That might hold them for a few minutes."

Just then, a series of little red bulbs in wire cages near

the ceiling flickered on. They were bright enough that we could see where we were going, but not so bright that anything was crystal clear. "Back-up generators," Dawkins said. "I was hoping they wouldn't have any of those."

Ahead of us was the top of a stairwell. Dawkins gestured for us to follow. "Nice and easy," he whispered as we made our way down in the darkness.

The stairwell opened on to a corridor. Far to our left was a pair of double doors like you might see in a hospital, with big square windows set into the top half. Through the glass we could see flickers of illumination – torches, maybe, or light from the back-up generator.

"Are they going to finish what they were doing to Sammy?" Greta asked.

"I don't think the back-ups can generate enough power for that device to work," Dawkins said. "The whole reason they need their own power substation is that the Eye of the Needle takes a lot of juice. So Sammy *should* be safe. For now."

Doors lined the corridor. "Ronan, about where was it that you saw Ogabe's head?"

I closed my eyes and tried to remember the distance

from the operating-room window that Greta had crouched over. "This one," I said, running to the second door along. "I think it's this one."

Dawkins tried the knob, then stepped back and kicked it open. "Inside, everyone. And no torches! Remember, there are windows in the ceiling." Once we were all inside, he eased the door shut.

Dawkins raised a finger to his lips. From the other side of the door, we heard the sound of feet pounding past. Someone was barking orders.

After they'd gone, Dawkins took the Zippo from his pocket and cupped his hand around it. In the bit of light he let escape between his fingers, we could see that the room might once have been a small office. Now it was a cell. The desk had been shoved against the wall, and in front of it was a bed.

Lying on top of the bed was the shaved head of a young black man. Its face grinned, and Ogabe's body pushed its way between the three of us, went to the cot and gently picked it up.

"Who's got the tape?" Dawkins asked in a whisper.

"Tape?" I said. "You never said anything about tape!"

"I'm sure I put a roll of duct tape on Gaspar's workbench when I grabbed the lock-pick set and screwdriver," Dawkins said.

"You only brought the screwdriver," Greta said. "There isn't any tape."

In Ogabe's hands, his head rolled its eyes. The hands shifted the head around until it was tucked into the crook of his left arm like a football, and then he turned his right hand in a gesture that clearly meant "proceed".

Dawkins sighed. "Sorry, friend. I got distracted."

The headless shoulders shrugged, but the face under its arm winked at Dawkins.

"I wonder where that goes to," Dawkins said, pointing to a door on the left wall. "Greta?"

She unrolled her lock-pick set and a few seconds later, we stepped through and into the office next door.

"Who's there?" asked a woman's voice as we came in.

Lying face down on the bed, hands cuffed behind her back, her feet tied, was a woman in old paint-spattered jeans and a men's blue button-down shirt. There were bruises on her face and a nasty-looking cut over her right eye.

My mom. My crazy intense, way-too-bossy, badass and brilliant mother, fearless protector of Greta Sustermann and my favourite person in the world. Her clothes were stained dark with something new – blood, maybe. And then I didn't see anything else because my vision got all wavery.

OK, so I was on the verge of crying. So what? Somewhere deep down I'd believed my mum was going to turn up dead. Without her, I'd be all alone in the world. I'd have my dad, but now I realized something I hadn't understood before: my dad just didn't count as much.

She flopped around until she could see us, squinting in the weak light from the Zippo. "Ronan?!" she said, disbelief and anger in her voice. "You should *not* be here!"

I tried to say, "Mom", but all that came out was a strangled noise, so I just dived down and hugged her. "You're OK," I finally managed to say.

"I will be once I get out of these cuffs," she said. "Why are you *here*, Ronan?"

"Hold on, Bree, while Greta unlocks you," Dawkins said.

"Greta is here too?" my mum said. "Greta *Sustermann*? I'm going to kill you, Jack!" She struggled for a moment, then relaxed so that Greta could pick the locks on the cuffs.

"Your threats scare me not at all," Dawkins said. "I've

been killed twice already since yesterday. I'll explain about the kids later, but trust me – they gave me no choice."

My mom said nothing, but gave Dawkins a look that I knew well – it said that death was the least of his worries. After a few moments, the second cuff rasped open and my mother sat up on the bed and hastily untied her legs. She stood and folded me into a crushing hug, then held me away and stared into my face. "You're OK?"

"I'm fine," I said. "Honest."

A flicker of light from above silenced us. "They're searching!" Dawkins hissed, dousing the Zippo. "Everyone against the walls."

We hugged the walls as the beam of a torch played through the glass panel in the ceiling. After a moment, it moved on.

"Did you find Dad?" I asked my mom once it was dark again. "Is he OK?"

Mom stared at me in the dark, then turned on Dawkins again. "Why did you bring the children?" she asked, despair in her voice. "This is the *worst* place. Do you know what they're doing here?"

"Sadly, yes," he replied. "We saw a demonstration a

few minutes ago, just before the lights went out."

She sniffed. "Why do you smell like something's burning?" Then she looked at Ogabe. "And what happened to his head?"

In the next connected office, a woman's shawl was draped on the bed, and a table held a glass of water with a lipstick smudge on the rim. Dawkins felt the bed and said, "It's warm. Whoever was here, we just missed her."

There were footsteps in the corridor outside, and someone tried the handle. We all froze. Apparently satisfied, the footsteps moved on. "When they try Ogabe's cell, they'll find our entry point," Dawkins said. "We need to hustle."

In the room beyond the office with the shawl, trussed up in much the same way we'd found my mother, a man lay on the bed.

"Dad!" Greta cried.

Gaspar Sustermann wasn't a big man, but he was broad-shouldered and muscular, and his receding red hair only made him look tougher, like a military man in civilian clothes. Greta hugged him where he lay on the bed. She pressed her face against his shoulder and said,

"I missed you so much! It's been a horrible day, Dad, first the train and the swords and then a truck ran over our friend and Ronan and I had to—"

"Honey," Gaspar Sustermann said, "it is great to see you and all, but can you do your old man a favour and open these cuffs?"

"Oh, geez!" Greta exclaimed, sitting up and dragging the back of her hand across her eyes. "Of course! Sorry!"

In the final, empty cell, Dawkins had Greta work the lock to the hallway while he quickly briefed Mom, Gaspar and Ogabe's head on what we'd seen. "This Eye of the Needle device is functional and they were planning to try it out on a few test souls – starting with this poor kid named Sammy. Then, I suppose, you two."

"Kid?" my mom said. "That doesn't sound right. They have a woman from Brazil, a Pure they smuggled in." She probed the wound above her eye and winced. "Unless you're telling me they have *two* Pure?"

"No, the boy isn't a Pure, he's just some foster kid who got caught up in this," Dawkins said. "We cut the power before they were able to hurt him. But if they have a Pure here, where is she?"

"That shawl," I said, remembering. "You said we'd just missed her."

"They must have had her ready for the Eye once they'd finished testing." Looking more worried than I'd ever seen him, Dawkins rested a hand on Greta's shoulder. "We need that door open now, Greta. We've got to get to this woman before they run her through that device."

"But weren't they going to run Sammy through it first?" I asked. And then, when I saw the look on Dawkins' face, I added, "Not that that's a good thing!"

"They know we're here," Dawkins said, "so they're not going to pussyfoot around with test subjects. They'll take the Pure's soul as soon as they're able."

"It's a good thing the power is out, then," Gaspar said.

There was a soft click and Greta cracked the door open an inch.

In the empty hallway, there was a flicker as the red emergency generator bulbs dimmed and went dark.

"What's going on?" I whispered.

Dawkins swung the cell door open, and we carefully edged out into the pitch-black corridor. "The only reason the emergency generator would cut out," he whispered, "is if—"

With a crackle of electricity, the hallway was bathed in white light.

The generators were back on.

CHAPTER TWENTY-SIX

THE EYE OF THE NEEDLE

Dawkins ran to the double doors at the corridor's end.

He threw himself against them, then fell back, saying, "Barred from the other side." Raising his fists, he slammed them against the wire-reinforced glass of one of the windows to get the attention of the people inside. "The facility is surrounded!" he shouted to them. "Stop what you're doing and come out with your hands where we can see them!"

"You brought help?" Greta's dad asked. "The place is surrounded?"

"No," Greta said, frowning and shaking her head. "Dawkins called somebody, but they were too far away to get here in time. We came alone."

"This is where one of those Tesla guns would come in handy," I said. I went to the other door and looked in.

The room was small. In its centre was the trolley, but now instead of Sammy, a woman was strapped to it. She was younger than my mom, but not by a whole lot. And she was obviously freaked out of her mind, looking from person to person, talking non-stop, probably pleading – though no one in the room paid her any attention.

At the foot of the table was Sammy's foster father, Dr Warner, and next to him the petite blonde woman who was his wife. Beside her was the Bend Sinister agent called Donald and another guy with dark hair and a goatee. They were holding on to Sammy, who looked terrified.

At the head of the trolley was a man I hadn't noticed from above, a man whose face was completely concealed by a red mask.

"What *is* that thing?" Greta whispered. "It's horrible!"

The mask *moved*, squirming on his face like it was alive, rippling and changing shape with each breath the man took. One moment it was long and narrow, the nose and cheeks pointy beneath writhing hair like barbed wire; the next, the nose curled in upon itself, flattened and disappeared entirely. Another moment, and the jaw and brow widened, thickened, the eyeholes vanishing into folds of flesh as the cheeks swelled up. The shifting never stopped, the mask slithering around the man's head like a living nightmare. Watching it squirm made me sick to my stomach, but I couldn't look away.

The only part of the mask that *never* changed was a large almond-shaped third eye just above the eyeholes. It was closed, but I could guess pretty easily what it was: the Perceptor. The neon-green eye Dawkins had told me was the Bend Sinister equivalent of a Verity Glass.

If the man in the mask looked at Greta with the Perceptor, I wondered, would he see the blindingly bright burning of her soul? Would he realize that my friend was one of the Pure he was looking for and come after her next? Would he kill her?

I shoved Greta away from the glass.

"Hey!" she griped, shoving me back. "What are you doing?"

"Sorry," I said, "but it's too horrible! I, um, can't bear to watch."

By that time, my mom and Dawkins had blocked her from view. "Ronan's right," he said. "This is exactly the sort of thing I wanted to protect you two from by leaving you in the car."

Greta's dad shielded her with his body, but I could still see. The man in the mask reached up and touched something on his face.

Slowly, the third eye inched open. It burned a sickly electric green.

My breath died in my throat. No wonder that foster kid had been terrified by this mask. No wonder Sammy was afraid of this guy.

Then our view was blocked by another face: Ms Hand.

She must have been inside the room the entire time. Smiling, she looked at each of us, and then she caught my eye. She mouthed a single word.

"What did she say?" Greta asked from behind me.

"Watch," I whispered. "She said, 'Watch.'"

She moved away in time for me to see Mr Warner administer an injection to the woman on the trolley – some kind of sedative, I guessed, because she quietened down and seemed to fall asleep.

Behind the woman, Mrs Warner moved to a control panel and flipped a lever. That searing net of red light again crisscrossed the Eye of the Needle. Dr Warner screwed the silver Conceptacle into place and the people around the trolley stood back.

"We can't just stand here!" I shouted. "We have to *do* something."

But it was too late. Dr Warner was already pushing the metal table through the Eye. As we watched in horror, the device did what it had been invented to do: it combed the woman's soul out of her body.

Whatever sedative they'd given her didn't matter: once the process started, she woke up and began thrashing and screaming as the trolley rolled through the hoop.

Sammy screamed, too – a long, wailing cry that made me want to cover my ears.

And then the woman's scream abruptly cut off and she went still, her back arched, a fine white smoke wafting out of her open mouth. She looked dead, but as we watched, her body slumped down again, and I could see her chest rise and fall as she breathed.

The Head raised a hand and closed the Perceptor, and Mrs Warner flipped the lever. The net of light in the hoop disappeared in a burst of static.

It had taken less than a minute.

While Dr Warner removed the Conceptacle and packed it into a padded steel container, Donald handed Sammy over to his foster mother. Mrs Warner pulled him in close for what might have looked like a hug if she hadn't just tried to sacrifice him. He struggled, but she clasped him tight.

"What's happening?" Greta asked from behind me.

"They took that woman's soul," I said. "They did it."

Donald and the goateed man carried the steel container through an open door on the opposite side of the room, while the Head, the Warners and Ms Hand watched them go. I pounded my fist on the glass, and the Head looked over and stared at me while the thing covering his face pulsed and contorted.

That was when Sammy broke free.

He bit his foster mother's hand, ducked past Ms Hand and threw himself at the door. There was the noise of a metal bolt moving, and something scraped away, and then Ms Hand was on him again. She gripped the back of his shirt and flung him backwards.

But he'd done enough.

Dawkins and Ogabe pushed open the doors, and the metal crossbar that had been blocking them clattered to the floor.

Backing away, Ms Hand shouted, "Go!" and the Head and the Warners fled out of the far exit, leaving Sammy behind.

On the other side of the trolley stood Ms Hand, the

blade of her drawn sword against the unconscious woman's neck. "Stop where you are or I will kill this Pure."

"Haven't you done enough to that poor woman?" Dawkins asked, but he did as instructed and paused mid-step. So did Ogabe.

Ms Hand beamed at me. "It was so kind of you to bring us Evelyn," she said. "I feared we'd lost him entirely, but thanks to you, my mission is complete."

"Why do you want to kill him?" Dawkins asked. "Why does a dopey thirteen-year-old kid matter so much to the Bend Sinister?"

"*Kill* him?" she said, and chuckled. "No, we never wanted to kill—"

Something struck her in the face.

Ogabe had thrown his head.

Ms Hand flinched and swatted at it, swinging her sword. In that moment, Ogabe's body swept the unconscious woman up into his arms and back-pedalled down the hall. His head rolled off the trolley to the floor.

"Bree, Gaspar, Greta," Dawkins said, "chase down that soul. Ronan and I will take care of business here."

My mom, Greta and her dad slid past Dawkins and charged after the Warners and the Head.

"You will be too late," Ms Hand said, coming around

towards us, slashing the air with her sword.

Her foot connected with something and she glanced down. With a cry of disgust, she swung back her leg and kicked Ogabe's head like a soccer ball. It bounced off the open doors and rolled after his body down the corridor.

"You have a longsword," Dawkins said, stepping around the table towards her. "And all I have are my good looks. Hardly seems fair to you."

"Come closer," Ms Hand said, jabbing the blade forward, "and we'll see how your looks fare."

"Tempting!" Dawkins replied. "Yet I think I'll decline your kind offer. At least until I've found some means of defending myself."

Ms Hand circled around towards Dawkins, stepping over Sammy where he was crouched in a ball on the floor, probably figuring the little kid was no threat to her – if she'd even noticed him at all.

And then he launched himself against the back of her knees in a flying tackle.

She grunted in surprise and flung her hands out to break her fall.

Her sword skittered away on the tiles.

Sammy was on it a moment later. Sword in hand, he

backed away from her. "Who's the boss now, huh?" he asked.

"Give that to me, little Samuel," Ms Hand said as she got to her feet. "It is not too late to make up with your parents. To prove yourself to them."

"*They* should prove themselves to *me!*" Sammy shouted. And then he tossed the sword toward me. "Ronan, catch!"

It wasn't a bad throw, but I never had a chance.

Ms Hand lunged sideways across the trolley, catching the sword by the hilt and sweeping the blade around to where my arm would have been if I'd reached for it.

I ducked and slid around the trolley to Sammy's side. "Sorry about that," he said. "Sorry about everything."

"Don't worry about it," I told him, leaning away from the point of Ms Hand's sword and pulling him with me. "Let's just back up until we're out of her reach."

"We've got nowhere to back up *to*," Sammy said.

We knocked against something bumpy. I felt around behind me — knobs and dials and a lever — the control panel. Nothing I could use to block Ms Hand's blade.

"I was never supposed to kill you, Evelyn," she said with that cold smile of hers. "But sometimes accidents happen." She raised her sword.

Behind her, Dawkins was working his way around the trolley, a metal surgical tray in his hand. But he was too far away to reach us, too far away to stop her.

I was unarmed, but *a Blood Guard finds weapons in whatever he has at hand.* So as she slashed down, I grabbed the only thing within reach.

The Eye of the Needle.

I swung it forward, and her sword bit deep into the segmented ring.

The blade stuck. Grunting, Ms Hand twisted it back and forth. Before she could pull it free, I realized that what was poking me in the back was the lever Mrs Warner had used, and I flipped it up once more.

The Eye of the Needle nodes lit up, and the web of red beams wove themselves through the empty space at the centre of the hoop. The guy who'd called it beautiful was on to something – up close, the crisscrossed net of brilliant light was like nothing I'd ever seen.

But then something went wrong. The beams began to stutter and break up, and tendrils of red light crackled out of the device like stray bolts of lightning, licking up along the sword blade and engulfing Ms Hand.

Her body went rigid, her straw-like hair standing

up straight, sparks of red chasing themselves across her teeth as she stared, grimacing, into my eyes. Her face and hands slowly grew brighter and hotter, until she seemed to blaze with energy, like the white-hot sword she still held. With a final sizzle, she burst into a coarse grey rain of ash and pattered to the floor.

With a loud, ragged gasp, I finally took a breath.

"Ronan?" Dawkins gently touched my shoulder. "You can turn off the juice now."

I cranked the lever back and it was over. The sword remained wedged in the Eye, electricity snapping from its hilt as it cooled.

Dawkins toed the ash pile. "Live by the sword, die by the sword," he said. And then he reached up and wrenched the blade free.

Sammy was trembling and wild-eyed. "She's gone?" he asked, gesturing at the ashes.

"I think pretty definitely, yeah," I said.

"Friend," Dawkins said to Ogabe, who stood in the doorway, holding the woman and his head in his arms, "I'm going to need you to stay here and make sure nothing else happens to this Pure. Ronan and I will go after her soul."

Ogabe gave us a thumbs-up.

"And Sammy? Greta? I want you to stay here with Ogabe."

Sammy looked at Ogabe, whose disembodied face gave him a grin, and said, "Sure, I'll stay here with Greta and the headless dude."

Just before we went through the door the Bend Sinister had taken, Sammy called out, "And Ronan? I'm really sorry about—"

But I never got to hear what Sammy was going to say.

The door led to a junction of corridors. At the centre was an empty reception desk and lying on the floor around it were several men in dark blue suits – men like Mr Four, though I didn't see him among them. It was pretty clear that they were all dead.

"What happened to these guys?" I asked.

"Their Hand – your Ms Hand – was broken," said Dawkins. "She was the only thing that kept them animate. When their Hand burned up, so did their life force."

Dawkins looked at his map. "There are too many corridors to search. We've got to split up. I'm guessing that shipping and receiving is the most likely place for them to depart from, so that's where I'll be headed.

Ronan, you go the other way. If you see them, don't engage, just come find me."

"OK," I said, and took off, running.

The corridor he'd sent me down ended at a stairway. As I started up it, the power went off again and I was plunged into darkness.

I crept along slowly, feeling my way up the steps until the back-up generators kicked in once more and the little red lights came on. At the top of the stairs was a door of reinforced steel – and it was slightly ajar.

I pushed it open and found myself in an unfinished passageway. The concrete walls were bare breeze block and the floor was steel decking. Behind me, the door swung closed, some kind of magnetic lock thunking into place.

But I wasn't really worried about that, because at the opposite end of the passage were five people I'd seen before: Dr and Mrs Warner, then Donald and Goatee Guy, carrying the case with the woman's soul, and at the front, leading them, the Head. Before I thought about what I was doing, I shouted, "Halt! Don't you take another step, or—"

The funny thing? They actually *did* halt – at least

for a moment.

"Or what? Are *you* going to stop us?" the Head asked, turning. "All by your lonesome?" That terrifying red mask was still squirming on his face, it's third eye open.

There were five of them and only one of me, and two of them – Donald and Goatee Guy – were armed with swords.

Me, I wasn't armed with anything. "Um," I said. "Scratch that. Feel free to proceed."

One of them heaved open the door at the far end of the corridor. The Head gazed at me, tilting his gruesome face. "This is the only way out of here, son."

I thought of the magnetic lock I'd heard snap into place behind me.

"Come now." The Head's voice was calm and smooth and weirdly familiar through the mask. "You and I aren't supposed to be enemies."

I looked around for something I could use to defend myself. There was nothing remotely like a weapon nearby, just a broom and a plastic dustpan.

The Head waved his companions on. "Secure that soul in the boat," he told them. "Donald and I will follow after we've taken care of this boy." Then he turned back to me, reached up and lifted the mask away. The creepy thing stopped moving as the Head's real face came into view.

He was an ordinary-looking middle-aged man, with a beard and close-cropped brown hair that was going bald on top. It would have been a relief to see someone so normal under the mask, except that now I saw the Head for who he really was.

My dad.

CHAPTER TWENTY-SEVEN

ALL IN THE FAMILY

"*You're* the Head?"

"Ronan!" He grinned and tucked the no-longer-alive mask under his arm. "I'm so glad you're here, son."

I wheezed, dizzy, unable to get enough air. Reaching out, I steadied myself with a hand on the wall so that I wouldn't pass out. "You're not kidnapped?" It didn't make sense. Mom had said he'd been taken by the Bend Sinister, hadn't she? She'd gone to rescue him. "But who trashed our house?"

He shrugged and said, "I was looking for some information that your mother had hidden. I wasn't as tidy as I might have been."

"The Pure," I said, thinking of Greta. "You were

trying to find the Pure she was guarding." The edges of my vision were darkening; I was hyperventilating.

His smile slid away and a hardness I'd never seen before settled into his features. "So you know about that?" He flexed his hands and looked down at his gold wedding band. "I always wondered how much your mother had told you about her work."

"I only found out about the Blood Guard yesterday," I said, still struggling to get my breathing under control. "When she picked me up from school."

"Yes," he said, his face lighting up with a smile again. "She got to you before me. I sent a team to fetch you — first at school, and then at the train station. You and your friends led us on quite a merry chase."

"That was you?"

"People working for me." He handed the mask to Donald, then held his arms wide. His voice was husky with emotion as he said, "Our family was broken and I wanted my son to be with me. I miss you. Is that so terrible?"

When he said that, an ache opened up in me that I hadn't even known was there. I missed him too —I'd been missing him for years. But then I remembered the bumpy flight down the park stairs, the sword fight on the train, the lorry rolling over Dawkins. Mr Four going after Greta with a hatchet. Izzy trying to skewer me. Ms Hand. Sammy about to be run through the Eye of the Needle. "Those people working for you tried to kill me."

"Not so!" he said. "Maybe it *seemed* like that, but trust me – their orders were to get rid of those with you, but to capture you with a minimum of injury."

"A minimum of injury," I repeated. *That* sounded more like my dad, the man who'd ditched his family to go crunch numbers as a comptroller. Though the minute I thought that, I realized his job was probably a lie too.

"I love you too much to let anything bad happen to you, Ronan," Dad said. "If you're not with me, then the work I am doing with the Bend Sinister means nothing. It's all for you – you represent the future."

The sad thing? I wanted to believe him.

My mom's pride in me was obvious in everything she said, but Dad's never was. His faint smile of approval was the thing I always wanted and almost never got. When I'd been little, we'd been pals, but that had changed a long time ago – sometime after my mom had started training me, I realized. Did she do that just because I got bullied at school? Or because she feared I'd one day face some other, bigger enemy? Not my dad, but the Bend Sinister – which, as it turned out, were the same thing.

"You may think I was dishonest about who I really am, but I wasn't the only one. Your mother has lied to you too. Do you think she truly didn't know who I work for?"

"If Mom lied," I said, "she did it to protect me from you." She hadn't gone after Dad to save him; she'd been trying to stop him.

And that was why Sammy had run from us on the highway, why he'd acted so strangely after we rescued him. He'd heard my name and recognized it – not the silly *Evelyn* that my mother had given me. But the *Truelove* I took from my father. The same name as the Head he feared so much.

The Head who had almost taken his soul just to test out a piece of equipment.

"You were going to kill Sammy," I said.

"Who?" he said, then shook his head, smiling easily. "Never mind. It doesn't matter. Come. Do as you're told. We are running out of time."

"You set the fire in Brooklyn," I said. I'd meant to ask it as a question, but as I said it I realized I already knew the answer.

"Ancient history," he said, waving it away. "You weren't supposed to be home. The whole idea was to make your mother crack and show us who she really was. We thought that by destroying her old life, we'd force her to lead us to . . . someone – her Overseer, another Guard, maybe even the one she guarded. But no." He rubbed his temples. "I wasted well over a decade in that marriage, and what came of it? Nothing."

What about me*? I wanted to say. I* came out of that marriage*. Or was I just part of his cover story too?*

My dad pulled back his cuff and looked at his watch. "We're out of time, Ronan. I'm afraid I'm going to have to force your hand." He motioned and Donald sauntered forward. An aura of pale pink light flickered around the long blade he held in his right hand, snaking through the runes carved in its steel.

"Whatever your mom told you about the Bend Sinister isn't true. We are going to bring about a new world, a better world. And I intend for you – my only son – to be a part of it. You know how much I love you, how much I've always loved you."

I stooped down and grabbed the broom and dustpan.

"You going to do some cleaning?" Donald asked with

a snort. He swung the point of his sword in little circles.

"We don't have to argue about this now." My dad pointed at my head. "The Perceptor reveals you do not wear the sigil. You're not one of the Guard. It's not too late to join us, not too late to make the right decision." He stretched out his left hand, palm up.

And that's when I knew: there was no decision to be made. I knew in my heart that my mom was one of the good guys. And so was Dawkins. And even if I wasn't an official Blood Guard with a sigil, I was a Guard where it mattered, in my heart.

My dad had stolen an innocent woman's soul, left her near death — and would do the same thing to thirty-five other innocent people if he could.

To Greta, if he knew what she was.

I threw the dustpan.

It whipped end over end, scattering dirt as it sailed right over Donald and caught my father square in the face.

He yelped and staggered back.

Rubbing his jaw, he said, "Donald, dispose of my one-time son and meet me at the dock." At the threshold, he paused. "I offered you your *life*, Evelyn. And how do you thank me? You throw a *dustpan* at me. A dustpan!"

He spun and stalked away.

"Don't call me Evelyn!" I yelled before the door hissed shut.

Donald's smile grew bigger as he strolled forward, as though he were coming to give me a hug, not skewer me.

"Well, Donald," I said, brandishing the broom, "what are you waiting for?"

With a roar, he lunged.

I let my training take over – the same training that had served me ever since my mom picked me up from school yesterday.

I caught him in the face with the head of the broom. He turned, spitting bristles, and I hooked his neck and yanked him off balance.

Then I planted the broom on the ground and pole-vaulted forward, throwing myself past him to safety. He swung at me with his blade, but I was already running down the hall, still clutching the broom.

"Hey!" he said. "Wait!"

I pulled the exit door shut behind me, and then turned the handle that locked it.

Yet another staircase took me up to a steel door with a push bar. I crashed against it and came out on to a concrete porch.

The blue-grey ribbon of the Potomac lay in front of me, glinting in the late-morning sunshine. To my left a concrete pathway led away from the building, snaking around the corner.

I took the path and came upon a hangar-like building set into a low hillside. It had a small loading dock with space for a truck, and a boat slip. In the slip was an open motorboat, and in the boat were the Warners, Goatee Guy and my dad. The case with the stolen soul sat beside him on the deck.

My dad looked up, saw me and shook his head, then turned away and started the engine. Goatee Guy threw off the mooring ropes, and without another look, my dad steered the boat out of the slip and into the river. I thought about throwing the broom I was carrying, but I couldn't imagine how it would do any good.

Instead, I watched until the boat was out of sight.

"Sorry, Mom," I said aloud. "I tried to do the right thing."

The harsh sounds of sword-fighting pulled my attention to the hangar.

I hadn't been able to stop my dad. But I could still help my mom.

I crouched down and edged along the loading dock to get a better look.

The inside of the hangar was empty – except, that is, for my mom and Greta's dad engaged in a fierce fight with five Bend Sinister agents. My mom had an enormous sword in her right hand, and every few seconds she would spin on one foot like a top, blurring in place, parrying the blades of the three agents attacking her, forcing them to fall back. Gaspar held a short sword in each fist, using one to block an agent while attacking with the other.

Watching from the edge of the dock stood a man in a dark suit. With one of his glowing gloved hands, he seemed to be conducting a tiny symphony, sweeping his fingers back and forth, curling them in upon themselves, flaring them outward.

A Hand.

A wild mix of emotions surged through me – pride in my mom, fear that she might get hurt, and above all, anger at my dad – that had me running forward before I knew what I was doing.

The Hand wasn't expecting anyone to be behind him.

I'm not much of a baseball player, but Mom had me in Little League when I was eight, so I learned how to swing at a ball. Gripping the shaft of my broom like a bat, I swung at the man's head as though I were swinging for the fences.

It was a solid base hit.

With a soft "Oh!" the man fell to the ground. At the same instant, the Bend agents around my mom and Greta's dad collapsed and lay twitching on the floor.

In the sudden quiet of the hangar, my mom called, "Ronan? Are you OK?" She dropped her sword and ran to hug me.

I let her. "You should have told me," I said against her shoulder. I felt her body tense. "About Dad."

"I'm sorry," she said, letting me go and stepping back. "I didn't know how. Things were already confusing enough, having to tell you about me and the Guard. If I'd also had to explain about your father and the Bend Sinister . . . well, I chickened out. I'm so sorry, Ronan." Tears aren't my mom's thing. She isn't the crying type, never has been. But I swear at that moment her eyes got shiny. "I messed up."

"When did you know?" I asked. "That Dad was part of this Bend Sinister thing?"

She stiffened, then said, "When was I *certain*? Yesterday. But after the fire I had strong suspicions that something wasn't right with your father. He has always been a little odd, but he'd become downright strange these past few years." She swallowed and looked away. "I *loved* him, Ronan. At least, once upon a time. Maybe that's why I was blind to what he had become. Or what he always was."

"OK," I said. I wasn't happy about any of it. Greta, Mom, Dad – no one was who they were supposed to be. "So all this time, he was one of the bad guys."

"One of the *worst* guys," my mom said, squeezing my hand. "Sorry, honey."

The doors at the back of the hangar suddenly banged open and Greta came running out. She embraced her father and then they got to work tying up the fallen Bend agents – the sort of father-daughter activity they did together all the time, I guessed. They'd nearly finished when Dawkins strolled out, leading Sammy and Ogabe, who still carried the Pure woman in his arms. Dawkins took in everything with a quick, wild-eyed look, then proclaimed, "Strong work, team!"

He drifted outside to where Mom and I stood in the sun. "I must tell you, Bree, your son has been truly heroic, and kept himself – and Greta – out of trouble."

"Did you know about my dad too?" I asked him.

He glanced at my mother and back to me. "Look, Ronan, your mother didn't know for sure – none of us did. But even if she *had* been certain, there is no easy way to give a boy that kind of news about his father. It would have destroyed you."

How *would* I have reacted if my dad had got to me first, before my mum? What if he'd told me about his work with the Bend Sinister, revealing that my mother was a liar and had a secret life? Would I have sided with him? Signed on for his vision of the world to come? Would I have felt for my mom what I now felt for my dad – that sickening swirl of disappointment, betrayal and fear?

Dawkins raised a fist. "Instead, she made you your own man. Gave you the means to make the right decision – Blood Guard or the Bend Sinister? – should you ever be faced with that choice. One that, as your mother, she never wanted you to have to make."

"I *am* truly sorry, Ronan," my mom said, looking straight into my eyes. "More than I'll ever be able to express to you. But I don't regret a single thing I've done."

"Nothing?" I asked, looking right back at her. "You named me *Evelyn*."

Mom smacked my shoulder. "Your great-uncle was

the best man I ever knew. *And* a member of the Blood Guard."

"You really need to get over that already," Dawkins said, smiling. "It's a *grand* name."

CHAPTER TWENTY-EIGHT

OUR FATES ARE DECIDED

A bit after that, Greta found me and asked, "Are you OK, Ronan?"

I didn't really know what to tell her. I wasn't hurt or anything, but I was confused and a little bit angry. I wasn't *OK* at all. Not that I could explain any of that to Greta. So instead I said, "I'm glad your dad wasn't hurt."

Her smile was big enough to make me forget for a minute why I was upset. "Me too! And I'm happy about your mum." She looked out at the choppy waters of the Potomac and asked, "Did she manage to find and rescue your dad? He's all right?"

"It was all a dumb mistake," I lied, turning away

from her and back to the hangar. "My dad was never in any danger at all."

Just then, a squadron of Blood Guard arrived in half a dozen white vans and saved me from having to say anything more. They were too late to rescue the Pure or to stop my dad from escaping, and for some reason I felt guilty about that – like it was all my fault somehow. The eighteen men and women were led by a cranky Overseer named Bruce, who barked orders while his team quickly cleared the facility.

"All of these people are part of the Guard?" I asked Dawkins when he came back out.

He shook his head. "They're not all Guard proper, no, but they . . . help us. Every organization needs people who keep the business organized – even a secret society of protectors."

They herded the bound Bend Sinister agents into one of the vans, loaded the comatose Pure woman into an ambulance and packed away the Eye of the Needle.

"I just pray we can find some way to reverse engineer this thing," Bruce muttered, scratching at his beard. "Because I don't know how long we can keep her alive without her soul. But if we can get this thing to put souls *back* into bodies, maybe we can undo what they've done." He scowled at the seven of us. "Dawkins, Ogabe. Truelove, Sustermann. No one blames any of you for what happened here today, but – how should I put this? – it was a complete and utter disaster."

"Yes, sir," my mom said. "Though I do—"

But Bruce talked right over her. "The Bend Sinister made off with this woman's soul. Their Head escaped. This Needle's Eye device has been ruined. That you're alive at *all* is more luck than anything else."

"We understand what you're saying, sir," Dawkins began, "but the situation—"

"The situation is as I've described it – a *mess*," Bruce said, glancing at his watch. "Debriefing is at the Arlington safe house at thirteen hundred. After that, we mobilize."

Bruce swung himself into the passenger seat of the lead van. As they began to roll away, he leaned out of the open window and said, "Oh, and Ogabe? Put your head back on. You look ridiculous."

We stood in silence as they drove off, all a little ashamed, I think.

All of us except for Dawkins. "That gives us two

hours," he said, breaking the quiet. "Anyone else hungry?"

Mr Sustermann drove us to the safe house in one of the white vans Bruce and his gang had left behind. The whole time, my mum and Dawkins argued about how best to reattach Ogabe's head.

"Glue won't do the trick," Dawkins said.

"I can sew a nice cross-stitch with some thread," my Mum suggested.

"Thread is *not* going to keep a massive head like Ogabe's in place," Dawkins objected. "We need something strong and durable so he can keep it together until the wound has sealed itself up."

So duct tape it was.

I wondered exactly how the smooth skin on the end of Ogabe's neck would reattach itself to his head, but no one else seemed worried, and before long we pulled into the driveway of a nice-looking two-storey house set back behind a line of trees.

In the garage, while Ogabe held his head in place, Dawkins wrapped his neck round and round with silver tape. He bit off the excess and patted down the end. "There you go! Good as new."

Under the tape, Ogabe's body parts sealed themselves with a disgusting, wet *slurp* sound.

"Wild," Sammy said in a hushed voice. "That's all you have to do? You're all better now?"

Ogabe grimaced and cleared his throat. "Hardly! I'll have to wear this tape for a week at least," he said in a voice that was a lot higher than I'd been expecting. He scratched under the edge of the tape. "And it itches something fierce." He looked at his reflection from a few different angles. "This looks *terrible*. How am I going to be inconspicuous with a band of tape around my neck?"

Dawkins put an arm around his shoulder. "My friend, you're six foot six and two hundred and eighty pounds. There is *nothing* you can do to be inconspicuous."

As if in argument, Ogabe's stomach growled.

"My thoughts exactly!" Dawkins said. "You don't have to tell *me* twice!"

"The big dilemma," Dawkins said half an hour later, wiping his mouth with a napkin, "will be what we do with you three."

We were sitting around a big trestle table inside the safe house, the remains of lunch in front of us.

"Normally," Mr Sustermann said, "you kids wouldn't be allowed to know about any of this – not the Blood Guard, not the Bend Sinister, nor any of our activities. What we do is secret and has been for centuries."

"It's a little too late for that now, isn't it, Dad?" Greta asked.

Mr Sustermann busied himself with his food, not looking up.

"There is a method by which the Guard can remove memories," Ogabe said, staring up at the ceiling. "It's not very, um, precise. In order to erase a few days, they have to blank out years."

"NO," Sammy said, standing up. "No way. My memories are the only place where my mom is still alive." He grabbed Greta's arm. "Tell 'em, Greta. Ronan? You won't let them do that?"

"Mom," I pleaded, catching her eye. "You *can't*. That's as bad as what the Warners were going to do."

"Everyone take it easy," Dawkins said. "Ogabe's not recommending anything. He's just telling you one method Bruce and the other Overseers may suggest. Me, I have other ideas." He smiled. "But first, Ronan, what do you think should be done?"

It seemed obvious. "We join the Blood Guard."

Mr Sustermann laughed as though I'd made a joke, but then stopped when Dawkins said, "Precisely!"

"Absolutely not," my mom said, pulling her eyes from me and glaring at Dawkins. "I can't believe you'd suggest that!"

"But Ronan's right," Greta said. "The only safe place for us is *in* the Guard. The Bend Sinister know who we are. They're never going to leave us alone."

"And me," Sammy said. "Don't forget me."

"Trust me," Ogabe said. "No one is forgetting you."

"Isn't this what you've been training me for all my life?" I said to my mum. I glanced at Greta. "What did you think was going to happen?"

"You're only thirteen," my mum said. Her voice was deadly calm – usually the sign a storm was about to be unleashed.

"And how old were *you* when you were recruited, Bree?" Dawkins asked her.

She said nothing, which I knew meant she didn't like what she'd have to answer.

"The Blood Guard is in a shambles," Dawkins continued. "Bruce told me we're not the only group attacked in the past twenty-four hours, and we can only assume the Bend Sinister has more dire plans afoot.

351

Our identities have been compromised. And we have allowed a Pure soul to be captured." He swept his gaze over everyone at the table. "There is a battle coming, and soon. We are going to need all the help we can get."

"I'm ready," I said, but Dawkins raised a hand for silence.

"*No one* is ready for what's coming, Ronan," he said, sighing. "Nonetheless, I'd rather we tried to make you three as ready as you possibly can be. Which means training. It won't be easy. In fact, more candidates fail than succeed. But that is what we can offer you – likely failure – if you want it."

"I do," I said, looking at my mom and daring her to tell me no.

She seemed to be evaluating me. After a moment, she nodded.

"That's what I want, too," Greta said.

Her dad and Dawkins exchanged a look, and I guessed what it meant: Greta was always going to need protection anyway; what better way than to surround her with the Blood Guard and to train her in their methods?

That or they were plain terrified of telling Greta "no" about anything. I know I would be.

"I want that too," Sammy said, sitting down again. "I mean, I don't want to go to another foster family. That has not worked out so well, if you know what I mean."

"The Guard can arrange a new family for you," Ogabe said. "One within the Guard. One where you'll be safe."

"Maybe," Sammy said. "I'll think about it and let you know my decision." He dropped his eyes to his plate and smiled.

"Fair enough," Dawkins said, clapping his hands together as a car pulled into the drive. It was Bruce and three others. "Time for our debriefing."

They made us wait in the living room.

Sammy, Greta and I waited on a couch, glancing back over our shoulders every now and then at the closed dining room doors where our parents, Dawkins and Ogabe argued our fate with the other four Blood Guard Overseers.

"Promise you won't let them mess with my head," Sammy said.

"They'll have to get through us first," I told him.

"Getting through *you* would be easy," he replied. "Greta is another story."

It was frustrating, sitting there. "Why is this taking so long?" I wondered. The longer we waited, the more likely it was that woman would die, or the Bend Sinister would capture another Pure's soul, or my dad would get so far away that we'd never stop him, or—

"Isn't it weird that my dad and your mom are both in the Blood Guard, Ronan?" Greta asked, turning to me. "Who do you think they're guarding?"

"Beats me," I said, thinking of the Verity Glass in my pocket. I'd have to make sure Greta never looked at herself through it. "Maybe they're not guarding anybody right now."

"Maybe it's *you*, Ronan," Greta said. "Maybe that was how you survived that fire in Brooklyn. Maybe the Blood Guard saved your bacon."

"Nope," I said, thinking of my dad and feeling my cheeks grow warm. "That was just dumb luck, plain and simple."

"And we know it can't be me," Greta said, scoffing. "I pick locks. I'm – I'm proud and sort of boastful. I even boast about boasting, that's how bad I am."

"You *are* pretty bad," I agreed, though I knew the Pure didn't lead perfect lives – but no need to tell Greta that. "I wonder who it could be?"

"Guys, isn't it obvious?" Sammy said. "It's *me*. My foster parents had me on that table and were going to run me through that Eye of the Needle thing."

"That's true," Greta said. "Maybe it *is* you."

"I totally bet it is," Sammy said. After a second, he said, "So what's a Pure?"

Dawkins' voice boomed out before I could respond. "Never mind that, Sammy. The question you all should be asking is, what comes next?" The doors to the dining room had opened and the eight adults had come into the living room. Greta, Sammy and I stood up together and turned. So this was it. Our fate.

"Sure," I said. "So tell us: what comes next?"

"Well, Ronan, Greta, Samuel," Dawkins said, raising his arms like a salesman about to make a pitch, "it's going to be a complete doolally, I'm afraid. You three will likely find it a little bit dangerous and a whole lot insane."

I grinned at him. "You're in luck," I said. "I'm perfect – *we're* perfect – for the job."

A smile broke out across Dawkins' face. "Exactly the response I expected," he said. "So gather round. We've got work to do."

ACKNOWLEDGEMENTS

If the idea of the Thirty-Six is even remotely real, then I've had the embarrassing good fortune to be surrounded by more than my fair share of these blessed people. Lucky me.

The following all deserve much more consideration than I could ever hope to fit on a single page:

Margery Cuyler, Kelsey Skea, Tim Ditlow, and Larry Kirshbaum of Amazon Children's Publishing — good-humoured trailblazers who take risks with new writers;

Melanie Kroupa, gentle editor of endless patience and perfect pitch, as well as Kerry Johnson, who repaired many unspeakably wonky sentences;

Alice Swan, Genevieve Herr, Stephanie Thwaites, Sam Smith and John McLay – UK stalwarts, pitiless in their smarts and sharp-eyed wit;

Ted Malawer and Ruth Katcher of the Inkhouse, both of whom give their everything in support of their writers and their stories;

Dan Bennett, Bruce Coville, Christopher Stengel – true friends all;

Beth Ziemacki, without whom, nothing.

Raoul, feline sidekick for nearly seventeen years. He passed away during the revisions on this book, and his absence is felt daily. Goodnight, little guy.

AN INTERVIEW WITH CARTER ROY, CONDUCTED BY JACK DAWKINS

ROY: Er. Excuse me. Can we get started?

DAWKINS: Do you mind? I'm just finishing my midday snack.

ROY: [sighs heavily]

DAWKINS: No need to get huffy. Let me just find my questions. [shuffling of papers] Right. Let's start with your height. You're a giant monster of a person, aren't you?

ROY: I'm six foot four. That's hardly monstrous.

DAWKINS: It's not just your height that seems monstrous. Perhaps it's your fishy pallor, or those enormous ears...

ROY: How about I tell you where I got the idea for *The Blood Guard?*

DAWKINS: Ah yes. You continue to insist that you came up with this story, when we both know that you're merely recording the true-life adventures of my friend Ronan Truelove. But do continue.

ROY: Like so many other ideas, it came from reading books, specifically one by Carol Matas that mentioned the *tsadkikim*, thirty-six pure souls.

DAWKINS: And what about the Blood Guard itself?

ROY: I thought, what would happen if those thirty-six were all taken out? Would the world end? Clearly, they would have to be guarded. But by who?

DAWKINS: By brave, fearless, dashingly handsome sorts! Selfless heroes!

ROY: Hm.

DAWKINS: So I take it you're a reader? That might explain your pale, pale, pale complexion.

ROY: It's winter. But yes, I am a big reader. Always have been. Books, I like to say, saved my life. I'm the youngest of five children who grew up in tough circumstances. Books and novels opened up a bigger world to me, gave me room to imagine a different life for myself.

DAWKINS: Reminds me a bit of a novel called *Matilda*.

ROY: Oh, yeah – Roald Dahl is one of my favourite writers from childhood. The first book I checked out of the library was *Charlie and the Chocolate Factory*. I could go on for pages about my other favourite writers—

DAWKINS: That's what I'm afraid of. Sometimes reading *The Blood Guard* feels a bit like watching a movie, with all the car chases. Why all the chase scenes in the book?

ROY: I sort of see the whole novel as one long chase,

with little breaks for comedy, character, and plot. A chase propels the storytelling and turns it into a breakneck thrill ride. Or at least, I hope it does.

DAWKINS: And your ideal getaway vehicle?

ROY: I'd love a jetpack.

DAWKINS: [scoffs loudly] They don't exist.

ROY: Fine. Then a really fast motorcycle.

DAWKINS: OK. Now we come to the big question...

ROY: Let me guess: Will I get you a sandwich?

DAWKINS: Will you? No? Never mind. My question for you is this: Would you rather be a Pure or a member of the Blood Guard? Would you rather live your life aware, or would you choose to be blissfully ignorant of your divine status?

ROY: [Excited] Are you telling me I'm one of the Pure?

DAWKINS: [laughing] You? A Pure? Ha.

ROY: Hmph. Well, I guess I'd rather be one of the Blood Guard. Though it doesn't seem like a long-term career.

DAWKINS: [his stomach growls loudly] Well, it's long past lunchtime and I'm bringing this interview to a close.

ROY: Wait – there's still loads I want to tell you about–

DAWKINS: Hang on – see those three over there? They look a bit like members of the Bend Sinister! What if they take us hostage and do unspeakably painful things to us? But they don't scare you, right? Because *The Blood Guard* is just a story, something you made up. It's just a figment of your— [sound of running feet and slamming door] Well, Mr Carter Roy has run out of the café. Interview finished. Time for lunch!